DEAD
DROP

A Jack Hunter Mystery

TO "BERMUDA BEV"

BEST WISHES

Robert Coburn

DEAD

DROP

A Jack Hunter Mystery
(Book 7)

Robert Coburn

ABSOLUTELY AMAZING eBOOKS

To Laura

Other books by Robert Coburn

A Loose Knot

A Deadly Deception

The Pink Gun

Little Boxes

Bad Tidings

An Evil Number

Malice Murder

A Rage of Deaths

DEAD
DROP

A Jack Hunter Mystery

A friend will help you move,
while a good friend will help you
move a body.

- Old Saying

Chapter 1

"I suppose I should feel sorry for him but he's not nice enough."

"He's a mean little shit, Candace," Amanda said. "You should kick him out."

"Yeah, I know but I loaned him some money. If I do that, he won't pay me back."

"How much does he owe you?" Drake asked.

"I don't want to say. It's too embarrassing."

Drake whistled.

"That much, huh? I'm with Amanda. Kick him out. Write it off as a bad investment."

Amanda and Drake Boynton were best friends with Candace Farrow. They shared a mutual interest and met regularly for drinks at a small bar on the Key West Bight.

"Soon as I get my realtor license it won't matter," Candace said, slurping the last of her pîna colada. "Sometimes I think he's from another planet."

"And I think we need another round," Amanda laughed.

Drake held up three fingers for the bartender.

"It's hard to even talk with him anymore," Candace complained. "Like we have different brains. I mean, look at the three of us. We're besties. It's almost like we know what the other is going to say before the words even come out. With Lee you never know what's coming next. Not that he'd ever say anything you'd want to hear."

The bartender placed their drinks in front of them.

"Here's to the three musketeers," Drake said, raising his glass.

Candace clinked her glass against his and Amanda's.

"I was just thinking about how we met," she said wistfully. "I was at this bar and Lee sat down beside me. He was kind of cute. We started talking. He asked what was I doing later. I said going to a lingerie party. Then for fun to see how he'd react, I explained how the *party* worked."

1

"That must've been an eye opener," Amanda laughed.

"Actually, he was very comfortable with it," Candace said. "Told me that he was into role playing. So we started seeing each other and sort of hooked up. Next thing, he moves in with me. And turns out to be the biggest jerk on earth with a temper to match."

"Oh, dear, has he ever hit you?" Amanda asked.

"One time after we'd had a couple of drinks and we were playing around, he started slapping me in the face. That really puts me over the edge. I told him to stop but he didn't. He just went on until he was ready to quit. Well, *he* knows better now. I just ignore him in about everything these days."

"Probably best," Drake nodded. "Never a good idea to go into anything after drinking. Too easy to make a mistake. But besides that, I have to tell you Lee Meadow never impressed me as being much of a gentleman."

"It's not his strongest suit," Candace scoffed. "Total asshole would be better fit. He's an abuser and a bully. Here's something you'll love. I've become friends with Karen Phillips."

"Wasn't she the nurse in that medical play?" Amanda asked. "She was really good. I liked the hygienic tips she gave each time she gave her partner a poke with the needle. Some were wonderfully funny."

"I've never gotten much out of those human pincushion acts," Drake said.

"Well, her partner recently moved off the island and she's looking for a replacement," Candace said. "I mentioned to Lee that I might be interested. Asked if he'd like to join us. You should've seen his face. Apparently, he has a real needle phobia. Probably cried his little eyes out as a kid when he had to get a shot."

They all laughed.

"By the way, Candace, Lee has a few things in my hanger," Drake said. "I'd like him to come get them."

"He's a hoarder," Candace said. "You should never have let him keep anything there."

"Yeah, well, I had the room and felt sorry for him," Drake said. "Tell Lee his crap has to be gone by tomorrow, otherwise it's in the dumpster. I mean it. Long weekend coming up and I don't want to spend it cleaning out the hanger."

"I'll bring him there myself to make sure. You can show me your new airplane."

Chapter 2

The pilot reduced power over Ft. Myers and twenty minutes later the Delta jet was rounding Sunset Key for the final approach into Key West International Airport.

Jack Hunter sat with his face pressed to the passenger window. He'd always enjoyed this part of the flight as the islands came into view and the waters shifted from blue to green – the shallows revealing a subterranean map of crisscrossing channels and sinkhole craters dotting the bottom.

It'd been a pleasant enough trip to Los Angeles but it had extended through the holiday weekend and now Jack was happy to be coming home. While he still had connections on the West Coast – both business and personal – Key West was the place where he'd finally taken root.

They were just passing over the last small, uninhabited key off Fort Zachary Taylor when he spotted a body tangled in the mangroves.

~~~

Detective Rachael Powers had been engaged in a civil conversation with her heart and her head while driving to work. The subject concerned commitments on both their parts. She was currently standing at a crossroads deciding which path to take, if either.

She'd arrived at the Key West police station without having reached a satisfactory solution for either side. Detective Earl Gleason was already at his desk.

"Good morning, sir," she called, entering the detective's room.

"Good morning," Gleason said, not looking up from the computer screen.

She saw that his coffee cup was empty.

"Get you another coffee, sir? I'm having one."

Gleason nodded.

5

"Anything interesting this morning?" she asked, returning with two cups. "Thought I'd drop by before leaving for my reserve training."

"Going over my report on that assault case before taking it to the district attorney," Gleason said.

"The idiot that beat up his girlfriend?"

"Yeah, a real sweetheart. Did a number on her. Ended up in the ER. That's why it's a felony and the DA gets the pleasure of his company. Long list of priors, too."

"Glad you handled it, sir. I might've stepped over the line with him."

"Sometimes taking that step comes close for all of us," Gleason said tight-lipped and hit the send key on his computer. He sipped his coffee and sat back in his chair.

"So, you still seeing our mutual friend?" he asked.

Powers felt herself blush. She wasn't in the mood for this juvenile game.

"If you mean Jack Hunter, yes, we do *see* each other occasionally."

Gleason smiled broadly.

"Well, I'd better get on the road," Powers said, finishing her coffee. "Long drive ahead. See you in a couple of weeks."

Gleason watched her leave and then returned to reading his report.

Lt. Jay Halderman was in his office on the phone with the front desk officer. A call had come from the Key West airport security regarding someone having spotted a dead body in the water. The man who'd reported it was there at the airport with them. The officer had already sent patrol and was just giving detectives a heads-up.

Halderman thanked the man and looked in the detective room. It was empty, save for Gleason who was sitting at his desk doodling on a piece of paper.

Fifteen minutes later Detective Gleason had parked in the airport lot and was inside the terminal. A security officer led him to a small room.

"This is the gentleman who reported seeing the body," he told him.

"Hi, Earl," Jack said.

6

Chapter 3

Jurisdiction in the Florida Keys is a complicated matter. Up to four separate agencies can be involved in an incident – Monroe Country Sheriffs, Key West Police Department, United States Coast Guard and the Environmental Protection Agency. Usually, there's cooperation between the offices.

This time KWPD won the coin toss.

The Coast Guard had accompanied the police motor launch to Archer Key south of Fort Zachary Taylor. Many of the uninhabited keys are named. A phone call to the EPA office in Miami had granted the police permission to circle the key but not to set foot on land. If that became necessary, they would have to send someone to observe. The entire area was considered a sanctuary, they'd reminded them.

Careful not to run aground, the small flotilla had drawn close to the key. Gleason could see no trace of a body in the surrounding mangroves. The wind had picked up and a strong current was running.

"Take it in closer," Gleason said, motioning with his hand.

The police boat nosed toward the vegetation; the Coast Guard remained behind in the deeper water. Gleason took out his binoculars and scanned the area along the entire side but again saw nothing.

"Wish I could wade around in there," Gleason said. "Have a much better look than from this thing."

"Sure we're at the right place, detective?" the officer handling the boat asked.

"According to the people at the airport, the plane would've passed over here," Gleason said. "Circle around the key."

They slowly motored around the tiny isle, returning to where they'd begun. Again, finding nothing.

About six football fields away, Jack stood on the rock jetty at Ft. Zach beach watching the action in the distance. After talking with Gleason, he'd gotten his Jeep out of hock at the

7

airport parking building and driven home to drop off his bags. Then he had continued on to the beach. His cellphone jingled.

"Hunter, there's nothing out here," Gleason said. "How many drinks did you have on that flight?"

"Not even one. I told you to let me come out there with you."

"Against regulations. This could've turned out to be a crime scene. You're fine where you are. Look, this *is* the key where you saw the alleged body, right?"

"As far as I can tell from here it is. The body was caught up in the mangroves on the side you're at now. I could see the legs sticking out in the water."

"Were there any boats around? Could it have been someone snorkeling?"

"It wasn't wearing swim fins and there were no boats. Maybe you should try a couple of the other keys farther out. I know we'd swung past Sunset Key and were lining up for the runway. I was trying to get the flight attendant's attention, but she was already seated."

Gleason ended the call.

"The wind has shifted since this morning," the officer noted. "Maybe it and the tide carried him off."

"Yeah, that's a possibility, assuming there *was* a body," Gleason agreed. "Too bad we don't have a helicopter available."

He thought for a minute then turned toward the Coast Guard boat.

"We're going over to that next key," he yelled to them. "Follow us."

It was the same story at that key and the next three as well. No sign of a body. Gleason decided to call off the search. The sun had begun to bear down harshly as it moved toward late afternoon and his life preserver chaffed uncomfortably. Also, his stomach felt queasy. As they headed back to the dock, one of the officers joked that Jack might've mistaken the dead man for a *man-a-tee*. Gleason didn't laugh. All he could think about was how smart the Sheriffs had been for not getting involved in this mess.

~~~

8

"Sure it was a dead man you saw, huh?" Billy Bean asked.

Jack had driven from Ft. Zack to the Inedible Cafe after Gleason had phoned him and told him they'd be in touch if there were any further need. His house was on a little lane off Olivia Street. Billy had at one time recommended it to him but he hadn't been interested then. However, he'd grown tired of Porter Court. Too many bad memories. And the house had come back on the market. He took it on a lease-to-buy deal.

"No question about it," Jack answered.

"A fellow I know thought he'd seen a dead man under his boat one time. Turned out to be a manatee come to scratch its back on the boat's bottom, hee, hee."

"I'm going out there myself tomorrow," Jack said. "Rent a boat and give the place a thorough look."

"Whole heap of ignorance out there, Jack. People in boats don't know what they're doing. Heavy current turning every which way when the tide's running strong. Might be getting some weather, too."

"Don't worry, I've been around boats."

"Let me get Sparrow to take you," Billy urged. "He's got a boat. Nice twenty-one-footer. Keep you safe and dry. Sparrow knows the water, too."

"Thanks, Billy, but I'll rent one from that place at the end of Duval Street."

"Speaking of Sparrow, hee, hee, you missed the excitement while you were gone."

"How's that?" Jack asked, knowing he'd regret it.

"Had to do with Sparrow's dad. Poor man's been getting a little off course lately. Sparrow stopped by to look in on him, see if he's okay. And there he was, naked as a jaybird running around the house flailing a machete over his head and yelling, "They're coming after me! They're coming after me!"

"What happened?"

"Well, they came after him, hee, hee. Took him to the hospital. He's doing okay now."

~~~

Key West was definitely in for a weather change. The next morning had welcomed a stiff wind out of the north that'd brought a ten-degree temperature drop. It was going to be a sweater day for those who might be lucky enough to own one.

The wind had also kicked up serious chop close to shore and whitecaps rolled farther out.

Detective Rachel Powers had driven into the bad weather an hour after leaving Lakeland at 4 a.m. It'd stayed with her almost to Miami before breaking off. Now it was again nipping at her taillights and, as she came into Key Largo, rain drops began splattering against the windshield. She switched on the wipers.

She was dressed in camouflage fatigues. That'd been the uniform-of-the day during the entire time she'd spent at the Army Criminal Investigation Department office, including the night before at the small ceremony when her new Captain bars had been pinned on by the commanding officer.

Traffic slowed and a microburst crossed the highway as the storm swept through. She pulled in at a restaurant parking lot and waited it out. As quickly as the downpour had rolled in, it chased off for the lower keys and Key West. Powers was on her way down US 1 again.

Passing through Big Pine, she noticed that the community had yet to fully recover from the damage Hurricane Irene had caused. Would it ever she wondered?

At last she arrived in Key West. The storm had already done its mischief there and had set its sights on the Yucatan. She drove to her house. It was early afternoon and she should check in with the department. A nap in bed took priority.

~~~

The paper had run the story about a local citizen having allegedly spotted a body but the police hadn't been able to confirm it. However, there'd been no boat rental for Jack to make his own search today. He hadn't even bothered to see about one. Even a landlubber like himself would've known better than to go out on the water in this weather. Instead, he'd futzed around the house taking care of a few odd jobs he'd put off for too long.

Painting the bathroom had been a snap, though messy. Replacing a washer in a dripping kitchen sink faucet had become another matter, however, when he'd stripped the threads on the hot water tap. The plumber couldn't come until tomorrow. So now he had no hot water.

His neighbor a couple of houses over seemed to be a jack-of-all-trades and might've been able to fix the thing. He'd met the guy at a street party their lane had held right after he'd moved there. Seemed everyone knew each other and kept an eye out. Jack had liked that about the place. It was one of the reasons he'd taken the house. However, he had found no one at home when he'd gone over and knocked on the door.

The idea of doing any more home repairs had lost its luster. The weather had slackened to a soft breeze and it'd soon be sunset. He decided to walk down to Mallory Square and watch the show. Something he hadn't done for ages.

The sunset celebration came into being sometime during the mid-Sixties. It usually kicked off about two hours before the last act, which was when the sun sank below the horizon and earned a round of applause for the effort. While it'd always been a one-man show, as far as the sun went, the stage was now shared by street performers, magicians, jugglers and vendors. Along with the usual assortment of Key West characters.

Jack's wanderings through the crowd had eventually led him to El Meson de Pepe and he'd stopped there at the bar to enjoy a mojito. There was a lively bunch inside. He should bring Rachel here some afternoon, he thought. It'd be fun. Suddenly, a burst of clapping, shouts, and cheers from the square announced that the day was officially done. The salsa band in the bar struck up a hot number.

Jack hung around a little longer and then left. It was still light and he strolled up Duval Street. Most of the hawkers had gathered up their goods. A few sidewalk stands were open. A guitar player outside the San Carlos Opera House bemoaned his lost shaker of salt. Jack's memory scrolled back to the time he and Brownie had played that very venue until the cops finally chased them off. So long ago, yet always close to mind.

He turned at Olivia Street and headed home.

Chapter 4

Rachel Powers had awakened to find that it was daylight. However, she'd quickly discovered it was also the next morning. Last thing she'd remembered was lying down for a short nap yesterday afternoon. She'd apparently slept through the night. She had to hustle if she was going to make it to work on time.

~~~

Petty Officer 2nd Class Bud Handy had left his quarters in NAS Truman Annex Beach with an early swim in mind. He'd expected to find the tiny beach empty at this time of the morning but he had been mistaken. A body had washed up during the night.

~~~

It was musical agencies again. Starting with Handy reporting to Naval Security in Boca Chica, who notified both the Sheriffs and KWPD. Since the body was found on Government property, the Sheriffs conceded jurisdiction to the Navy, who decided it might be better to just let Key West PD cover the investigation. And the music stopped there.

Gleason and Powers stood on the sandy beach next to the body.

"Where're his clothes?" Powers asked.

The dead man was nude and lying on his stomach, his head canted to one side.

"Maybe he was skinny dipping," Gleason answered dryly.

"He doesn't look too good," Powers noted. "Wonder how long he's been in the water?"

Gleason knelt beside the body.

"Pretty nasty blow on the back of his head," he said.

Powers stooped for a clearer view and took a picture of it with her cellphone.

"Could've been why he drowned, sir," she said. "Hit his head on something and fell overboard. That is, if he was on a boat by himself. Still doesn't explain why he isn't wearing any clothes."

"Some people sail in the buff," Gleason said.

Powers found the idea of that appealing.

"I can see doing that," she said, getting to her feet. She automatically placed her hand in the small of her back. Old habit from an old injury that'd thankfully healed.

"You talked with our mutual friend?" Gleason asked.

Powers laughed.

"Funny you should ask," she said. "I got in yesterday afternoon and was so beat I took a nap. Didn't wake up until this morning. But to answer your question, no, I haven't spoken with anyone. Well, other than you and the lieutenant."

"Well, here's another funny thing," Gleason said. "Jack Hunter reported seeing a body on one of those keys out there. Said he'd spotted it from the airplane he was in when it was landing."

"You're kidding."

"I only wish I were kidding. But we took him at his word and searched every damn key this end of the island and found nothing. I figured he'd probably had a couple of drinks. Saw a manatee. Or maybe a mermaid. But now, what do you know?"

"I followed that storm all the way down the keys, sir," Powers said. "It was pretty strong. Maybe it washed the body he'd seen onto this beach."

Gleason considered that.

"Yeah, I just hate to admit Hunter was right," he said and then blew his nose. "Think I caught a damn cold being out on that boat. Don't see how. It was hot as hell."

"Are you taking anything for it?"

"Naw, I'll shake it. Minor stuff."

"I think the coroner's team is here," she said, seeing two men coming toward them carrying a gurney.

The body was bagged and taken to the Lower Keys Medical Center morgue. Gleason and Powers left for the police station to write up their report. There was no need for them to stay around any longer. The beach was obviously not a crime scene.

~~~

"Aren't you being unfaithful?" Powers asked.

"What?"

"Bringing me here. Does Billy know you go to other restaurants?"

Jack laughed.

"Always good to keep an eye on the competition," he said. "Besides, I just thought something different would be nice to welcome you home."

They'd gone to the Cafe Sole for dinner. The little restaurant, tucked away in Old Town, was a favorite with Jack.

"What do you recommend?" Powers asked, sipping her wine and picking up the menu.

"I was thinking about the shrimp," Jack said, "but the hogfish is terrific, too."

Powers put down the menu.

"So my partner tells me you sent him on a wild goose chase and he got seasick," she said.

"It wasn't a wild goose chase," Jack said. "I saw a body."

Powers glanced around the room and then leaned closer to him.

"Well, we found a body," she whispered. "Maybe it's yours."

"I knew it!" Jack exclaimed.

Powers shushed him.

"Don't know if it's the same body you saw," she continued, "but the odds *are* in your favor."

"Where was it?"

"Truman Beach. Do you know where that is?"

"Not really."

"Out by Fort Zach. Belongs to the Naval Air Station. The body had washed up there. I mean, we're assuming it did because there's nothing to indicate otherwise."

"Was it a drowning?"

"Waiting for the coroner's report. I just wanted to let you know that you weren't crazy. You ready to order?"

"No, wait a minute. I want to know more about the body. Was it a man or woman? Have you identified it?"

"All I can tell you is that it was a male. He had no ID on him."

She didn't mention he had no clothes either. Nor say anything about the suspicious head injury. In truth, for all she knew at the moment, that could've resulted from an accident. Her gut, however, told her differently.

"Okay, Jack? Now can we please order? I'm hungry."

Jack signaled for the waiter. Powers opted for the hogfish. Jack went with his first choice, the shrimp special. Both ordered another glass of wine.

"Here's to the new Captain Powers," Jack said, lifting his glass. "Gleason know you outrank him now?"

"I've haven't told anyone at the station," she said. "Actually, it isn't any of their business."

She also hadn't told Jack the complete story behind her promotion and how it could affect both of them.

"I never asked you about your trip to LA," she said. "Everything okay back there?"

"Just taking care of some business," Jack said. "Had to stay longer than I'd expected but all's well and good. Can't say the same for my place here. Plumbing's out. No hot water."

"Umm, cold showers, huh?"

"They can be invigorating."

"It's tempting, considering the company, but I have a big day tomorrow. Can I have a raincheck?"

Chapter 5

Gleason checked his wristwatch. Twenty-nine minutes on the button. If he could maintain the pace, he'd be looking at a personal best. He turned around and headed back. He'd been out since before sunrise.

He'd taken up running a few months ago. Actually, he'd been looking for something. The theater, which had been an earlier love, had fallen out of favor for some reason. So, starting out at about ten miles a week, he was now doing thirty. He had set a loose 10K course for himself, figuring it was three miles, give or take, from his apartment to the airport. The average time for a 10K race was fifty to seventy minutes. Top guys can pull it off in under thirty minutes.

This whole business had started with his cutting back on drinking. He'd limited himself to having an occasional glass of wine when he was out and kept nothing at home. His bank account had seen an immediate improvement. And he'd begun to feel better physically soon afterwards and decided to get in shape. Becoming a gym rat had held no appeal. However, he had noticed people running on the sidewalk along Smathers Beach during early morning. He thought he'd give it a try. Now he was hooked.

To his surprise, he'd found the small community of runners to be a welcoming group. There were men his age, some younger and others older. And women. All of them at different levels of the sport and most able to leave him in their dust. That could soon be changing.

Though he'd given a final kick on the last leg of the run home, it'd taken him nearly forty minutes to complete. Still, he was under the average time for a 10K and there'd been a couple of holdups at traffic lights. And that damn cold had slowed him down. Still, he was indeed improving.

Mitts greeted him at the door with a peal of meows.

"Can you just hold on for one minute, please," he said, pulling off a sweaty tee-shirt.

The cat had once belonged to the victim of an unusual homicide he'd investigated. He'd adopted it, or vice versa. It had six toes and was rumored to have been a Hemingway cat. The name had been his idea.

Having stripped down and with Mitts fed and purring, he showered and dressed for work.

~~~

"Any word on that drowning vic?" Jay Halderman called out from his office.

Powers had just walked into the detective's room. She stopped and stuck her head in the doorway.

"Probably too early for a cause-of-death ruling, sir," she said. "The victim only checked into the morgue yesterday."

"Yeah, I know," Halderman said. "Coroner's busy as hell with that shooting up in Marathon. Still, the heat's already on. Started soon as the paper ran the story. Drownings are bad for business, you know. The big hope is it didn't happen on one of our beaches. Floater coming in from somewhere else apparently is okay. What about identification? Know if he was from around here?"

"No hits on his prints so he doesn't have a record. That just covers Monroe County, of course. Don't have access to every town and county. Could even be he's from out of state. And if he's military, forget it. They don't share. DMV's been a little slow. I'll check with them as soon as I get to my desk. Also, I'll phone the coroner and see where they're at."

"No, let Dr. Harding do his thing," Halderman said. "Amazing how your friend Jack Hunter was right all along, huh?"

My *friend*, Powers thought to herself. At least he didn't add *boy* to it. She smiled and went to her desk.

Gleason hadn't arrived yet and she took the opportunity to go over the notes she'd taken at the scene. Also, she looked at the photos of the victim she had grabbed with her cellphone.

Of particular interest was a closeup of the blow to the back of his head. It just didn't look like something that might've been accidental. Say, striking a railing or being hit by a sail boom. She'd seen that happen in a movie once. The sail had

18

swung around and knocked a guy overboard. She didn't remember what movie it was. Some late-night thing. Also, he'd had on his clothes. Obviously, not into buff sailing.

No, this injury was no accident, she was certain. Whether it was the cause of death though would be something Dr. Blake Harding would have to determine.

Her computer pinged, announcing an email from DMV.

~~~

Jack had shivered through an ice-cold shower. But the thought of having to shave with the same freezing water had been too painful to even consider, so he'd heated a pot of water on the stove and dumped it in to the bathroom sink.

The plumber had called earlier saying that he couldn't come until sometime later that afternoon. An emergency job on Stock Island, he'd explained.

How long could it take to replace a faucet? Jack had wondered after talking with the man and considered just doing the job himself. Better judgement prevailed on second thought and he decided to take a walk instead.

Key West holds a special beauty in the early morning hours before the sun punches in for the day. Most everything is in shade, the air still and temperate. Traffic practically nonexistent, both on the streets and sidewalks. This time doesn't last for long and while it did Jack just followed his feet.

Olivia Street led him to Galveston Lane which he took to Angela and then cut up to Passover by the cemetery. From there down Margaret to Fleming and back to the library where he knew a bench would be waiting in the little tree-filled park next to it.

The bench was empty and Jack welcomed the opportunity for a rest. Save for some twittering birds and a couple of chickens scratching beneath the scrubs, he had the place to himself.

He looked around, taking in the peacefulness. It was almost as if the library extended its quiet rule out to here. He liked the idea of that.

He thought about his situation with Rachel Powers. How they'd become involved. Neither one of them looking at the moment. Just happened.

Lately, he'd even been considering asking her to move in with him. That would be a pretty big step. Was he really ready? How would she feel about that? He didn't want to push her. Things were fine now. Don't screw up.

Well, at least wait until he had hot water.

Another person entered the park. A little old lady with a large old dog on a leash. She ambled over to where Jack was sitting.

"Good morning, ma'am," Jack said. "Nice day."

She didn't answer. Jack noticed she was wearing earbuds. He also figured she must be stone deaf, or soon would be, because he could hear the music blaring from them. Solid rock and roll. She eased herself down on the bench while the dog gently lowered itself onto Jack's foot, pinning it to the ground.

Eric Clapton blasted out *Layla*.

Chapter 6

"Lee Meadow, sir," Powers said, holding a printout of a Florida driver's license. "Took forever but here he is. Shows an address on Duncan Street. Think that's in New Town. Also, he drives a 2005 Ford 150 pickup. Has a vanity plate...WHIPIT. Sounds like a breed of dogs. Maybe he raises them or something. Possible lead."

"Don't you live near there?" Gleason asked.

"No, my house is on Harris."

Gleason had just arrived at the station.

"Photograph doesn't favor him," he said.

"He wasn't dead then."

"Guess that'd do it."

"That injury on his head bothers me," Powers said. "What do you think?"

"Depends on what the coroner says. Let's check out Duncan Street."

The address was a small two-story apartment building. A rental sign stood in the front yard. Gleason parked on the street a little beyond it.

"I don't see any truck," Gleason said sniffling as they walked back.

Powers looked at him with concern. Was that cold contagious?

"Sounds like someone's home in the lower apartment," she said. "I hear a TV."

Gleason rang its doorbell.

"God, I hate this part," he said.

A woman in her late twenties answered.

"Good morning, ma'am," he said, showing her his ID. "I'm Detective Earl Gleason with the Key West Police Department. Are you Mrs. Lee Meadow?"

"No, I'm Susan Kirby," she smiled.

"Does a Lee Meadow live here?"

"I don't know any Lee Meadow."

Robert Coburn

A small wave of relief swept over Gleason. At least he didn't have to give the bad news to this woman.

"How long have you lived here, if I may ask?"

"We moved in six months ago. My husband works at the Naval air station."

"What about your upstairs neighbors?"

"They moved out last month. That's why the sign's there."

"Had they been here long?" Gleason asked.

"They were here when we came."

"You wouldn't know where they moved?"

"I think they said something about going back to Virginia. You could ask the rental company. Maybe they'd know."

"Well, thank you for your time, Mrs. Kirby," Gleason said.

"That's okay. Has this Lee Meadow person you're looking for done something wrong? I mean, should I be worrying if he shows up?"

"No, nothing like that."

She shut the door. Gleason heard the chain lock slip into place.

"Seems Mr. Meadow hasn't bothered to file a change of address with the DMV," Powers said, as they went to their car. "Not very civic minded."

"You got no hits from AFIS?"

"The national database doesn't have anything." Powers said. "Definitely nothing with us. And as I told the LT, the military doesn't give out its records."

"Okay, then onward to the rental agency," Gleason said. "Find out when he last lived at this address and maybe they'll also know where he moved."

"We could phone, sir. Save a trip."

"Always more fun face-to-face."

Powers smiled. She thought so, too.

~~~

"Should've called me, Jack. Plumber's just ripping you off. How much is he going to charge?"

After leaving the park, Jack had wandered over to the house on Ashe Street to visit with his old friends, Ruth LaVere and Bobby Sunshine. He'd mentioned his hot water problem to Bobby.

22

"Sixty bucks an hour is the plumber's going rate," Jack said.

"Piracy!" Bobby snorted. "And you can bet he'll take two or three hours to do a fifteen-minute job. Hell, all my tools are on the boat. C'mon, let's go. We can stop by Strunk's hardware store on the way to the marina and buy a new faucet set. Might need to grab a few other things while I'm there. I'll leave Ruth a note, though she'll probably still be at the beauty shop when we get back. It'll be good to get away from Roy for a little while, too. Parrot's driving me crazy with all this coughing and hacking."

Ruth had earlier suffered from a cold that'd settled in her chest and had given her a week's worth of coughing fits. Her African Grey parrot, who sang old standards but was ever on the lookout for new material, had added them to his repertoire.

"I walked here, Bobby. Look, there's no need for you to bother. Let the guy do what he does."

"Foosh, Jack! Run home and get that Jeep. I'll have you in hot water in no time flat."

~~~

Gleason and Powers had learned from the rental agent that Lee Meadow had skipped out with eight months still on lease. They'd tried to locate him but without luck. The agent had no idea where Meadow was now living. The detectives hadn't bothered to mention that Lee Meadow was no longer living, period.

"It bugs me that we can't get a handle on this guy," Powers said, as they drove back to the station. "Maybe someone will recognize his picture in newspaper. Girlfriend, boyfriend, whatever. I mean, he *did* live in Key West after all."

"Don't be surprised if we hear nothing," Gleason said. "People don't want to get involved these days."

"That's sad but I know what you mean, sir. Of course, on the other hand it could be prosopagnosia run amuck."

"How's that again?"

"Prosopagnosia, sir. Not being able to recognize faces. Everything else with your brain is okay, just can't handle faces."

"That happens to everyone occasionally, even me," Gleason said. "And now they've got a name for it? You're pulling my leg."

"It's a real deal, sir. There's been a study. Two percent of the whole population have some degree of face blindness. And worse in some cases. I'm talking about not even recognizing family members. That's how bad it can get."

"How do you know this stuff?"

"Just things I pick up in books and the newspapers. It's amazing what you can learn from reading."

They rode on in silence for a couple more blocks.

"We've done about all we can for the present," Gleason said, as they pulled into the lot. "We don't know if a crime has been committed. And until we find out otherwise, this is an accidental death."

"I'm counting on having the picture of victim in the paper to bring in something," Powers said.

"We may have to sell the brass on running it before the family's notified."

"Maybe he doesn't have any family," Powers said. "Besides, they've already published a story on the drowning. The picture's all we have at the moment, sir."

"Don't worry. It'll get done."

Chapter 7

"**C**andace just called," Amanda said, stepping out onto the patio. "She's upset about that body they found at Fort Zach. For some reason, she's afraid it could be Lee."

Drake and Amanda were at their home in Casa Marina. He was seated in the patio by the pool reading the newspaper. Barely waist-deep, the pool had been designed mainly for decoration. Irregularly shaped and surrounded by lush foliage – some plants even dipped into the water. It was really impressive.

"We need to get the pool guy over," he said. "The thing's bubbling again. I think it needs a new pump."

"I'm worried about her, Drake. She sounded so, I don't know, panicky. Maybe she shouldn't be there alone."

Drake refilled his cup from an antique silver coffee pot.

"Tell her she's welcome to stay with us anytime she wants," he said. "As far as that body goes, it hasn't been identified. Probably just some doofus who fell overboard after drinking too much. No cause for her to worry. Has nothing to do with anything."

"I'd hoped that little trip she took up north after Lee moved out would've helped but I guess not," Amanda said. "To tell you the truth, I'm surprised she's still moping about him walking out. You'd think she'd be dancing in the street to be rid of him."

"Well, here's a thought that might cheer her up," Drake said. "There's a social in Miami tonight. Monthly gathering for a meet-and-mingle. Why don't we all drive up? Take the Lexus. Might be fun for her to make some new friends."

"Oh, good idea and it's not dressy. I'll call Candace."

She came closer to where he sat and leaned down.

"Have you been a bad boy lately?" she whispered in his ear, placing a hand on his inner thigh.

"I've been a very bad boy," Drake said, moving her hand up.

25

"I believe some punishment might be necessary," Amanda said, straightening. "I think you should go to your room. I'll get dressed."

~~~

"You bought the wrong size," Bobby grunted. "This damn thing doesn't fit. Have to go back to Strunk's. Take the old one with us so we'll get it right this time."

"I didn't buy the fixture, Bobby" Jack said. "You picked it out. Said they were all the same so it didn't matter. This new thing even has a rinse hose. Do we need that?"

Bobby Sunshine was flat on his back beneath the kitchen sink trying to attach the new faucet water lines. He'd been at it for nearly an hour. Water was all over the place.

"The threads on the pipe are stripped, Jack," he said. "That's why it leaks every time I turn the water back on. You must've cross-threaded them. Need to clean 'em up. We can buy a thread cutter while we're at the hardware store, unless you have one."

"Why in the hell would I have a thread cutter, Bobby?" Jack asked, his patience on empty. "I thought you knew about plumbing. Didn't you do all of it on your boat?"

"Dad took care of that and the electrics. I did the cabinet work. Told you right after we first met I was a carpenter. You must not have been paying attention. Do know a little about motors. Next time that Jeep needs a tune-up, keep it in mind."

"Look, Bobby, thanks for the help but I'm going to call the plumber. Maybe he didn't pick up another job and I can still get him."

"Don't suppose there's a cold beer in that refrigerator?" Bobby asked wearily, struggling to get to his feet.

Jack got out two beers and popped them open.

"I suspect you've got yourself something exotic here with this fixture," Bobby said, after taking a long pull from the bottle. "That plumber of yours might be able to figure it out. With all this tariff business going on, no telling where stuff comes from anymore. Could be anywhere. Use a whole different standard of measurement. Look at England. Everything's left-handed there. Which reminds me about this

King Charles dog one of Ruth's friends has. You familiar with that breed, Jack?"

"Can't say that I am," Jack said, realizing what an idiot he'd been for involving Bobby in the first place. And that he'd most likely be spending another night without hot water.

"Smartest dog I ever saw," Bobby said, suppressing a burp. "Rings a little bell when it needs to go outside and pee."

"I don't believe it," Jack chuckled. "How's that possible?"

"The lady trained him," Bobby said. "Tied a little bell like the kind you'd put on a cat's collar to a length of ribbon. Then she pinned that on the door so it hung down to where the dog could reach. Every time she'd take him out to do his business, she'd shake the ribbon and the bell would give a ting-a-ling. Dog put two and two together and learned to nose the ribbon. Pretty soon all she had to do was come and open the door whenever she heard the bell ring."

"So how'd he get back inside?" Jack asked.

"Had another bell outside the door. You ready to run me home?"

~~~

Jay Halderman had expressed grave reservations about placing Lee Meadow's picture in the newspaper without having first notified the next of kin. However, given the fact that Mr. Meadow quite possibly had no other family, or at least none the KWPD could find, he'd reluctantly signed off. Gleason and Powers had been elated. At last, maybe they could get this case moving.

"Key West man found dead on beach," Powers read aloud from the front page. "Skinny dipping suspected. Police request assistance from anyone who might know something. Don't be shy, folks. Detectives are standing by to take your call.""

She and Gleason were at their desks.

"Gimme that paper," Gleason smirked.

He perused the story.

"They left out 'calling all cars'."

The phone rang.

"Homicide, Detective Gleason..."

"Gleason, this is Jack Hunter. The guy in the paper that drowned was my neighbor. Lived a couple of houses down."

~~~

Gleason and Powers had driven to Jack's after talking with him on the phone. Jack pointed out the house where Lee Meadow had lived and, leaving their car parked at Jack's, the two detectives walked to it.

"Not sure you should've said anything to Hunter about Meadow on your date at the restaurant," Gleason said.

Powers turned to him.

"My... date...," she repeated slowly. "I'll let that pass, sir. However, I saw no harm in telling Jack Hunter that he'd been right about what he saw. And now he's come forward again, right? What is it between you two?"

They stopped at the house. It was a single-story cottage with a porch running across its front and down one side to the entrance.

"I don't see any truck," Powers said, looking around.

"Let's go knock on the door," Gleason said.

No one answered. Powers peered in the window but could see no movement.

"All right," Gleason said. "We'll try the back."

The backyard held a deck and a hot tub. Some of the plantings looked as if they'd been broken. They returned to the front, where the next-door neighbor stood waiting on the sidewalk.

"Can I help you with something?" the man asked suspiciously.

"Perhaps so," Gleason said, flashing his police ID. "We're trying to get in touch with the person who lives here. Not sure of the name we have."

Jack had already given them as much information as he knew but it was always better to play a little dumb.

"That would be Candace Farrow. It's her house. Is there a problem?"

"No problem at all. We're investigating an accident."

"Gee, I hope Candace wasn't hurt. I was just speaking with her the other day. Or maybe it was earlier. Can't say for certain. Time passes so quickly nowadays."

"As far as we know, the lady is fine," Gleason said.

"That's good to hear. She's a divorcee. She and her husband moved to the lane about three years ago. Jerry Holtz. Nice guy but the divorce was kind of nasty. She got the house and he got to pay alimony. Ain't that the way it always goes?"

Gleason gave a tight little smile. He knew from his own experience that it went that way.

"And you are ...?" he asked.

"I'm Victor Young," the man told him. "Excuse me for not introducing myself. Lived here nearly five years now. I worked for an investment firm in New York. Handled mostly commercial real estate. One winter we had nothing but snow. I mean, everybody was freezing his ass off. Here it was the middle of April and still snowing. Wife and I lived in Jersey. We were empty nesters. Anyway, my office was in midtown on Forty-second Street across from Bryant Park. I was looking out the window right after another snowstorm. Took two hours to get in that morning. And this guy was down in the park stamping out letters in the snow. Big letters. What he finally wrote was 'FUCK THIS'. Best performance art I ever saw. Decided right then and there to quit the rat race and move to Florida."

Gleason had no idea why the man was sharing this, but it was obvious that he liked to talk. He'd bet he was nosy, too. He decided to encourage him. Sometimes you learn things you never would have otherwise.

"Sounds like you made the right choice, sir," Gleason smiled. "Kids still live in, where did you say, Jersey?"

"Son's in the Navy. Our daughter's married and lives outside D.C. Wife's up there visiting her now."

"So you're batching it, huh?" Gleason chuckled. "Look, I'm puzzled about this address. Did Miss Farrow ever rent out rooms? The reason I'm asking is we have a Lee Meadow listed as living here."

Young gave a sarcastic laugh.

"Yeah, he lives here" he said. "Haven't seen him around lately, though."

Gleason exchanged looks with Powers. Obviously, the neighbor hadn't read the morning newspaper.

"Now I understand," Young said, snapping his fingers. "He's the one that had the accident. That'd explain why his truck's been gone. I was hoping he'd moved out."

"Why is that, sir?" Gleason asked. "Was he a bad neighbor? You two ever argue?"

"No, I'm pretty easy-going. Thing that gets me is he's a slob. Piles up junk in the back. Place always looks like hell. Not very sociable, either. Frankly, I don't know what Candace sees in him." Then he added slyly, "Birds of a feather, I guess."

"How's that?" Gleason asked curiously.

"You know," Young answered, lowering his voice to a whisper and cutting an eye toward Powers. "Kinky stuff."

She took the hint.

"I'm going back to check on the car, sir."

"What kind of kinky stuff?" Gleason asked the man conspiratorially, after Powers had left.

"He'd tie her up and then they'd fool around," Young grinned. "They never closed the blinds so I couldn't help but see, you understand. It was the same thing when she and her hubby were together."

"Well, that's not against the law."

"Yeah, but he started slapping her around. Looked pretty hard, too. I could tell she didn't like it."

"Lee Meadow hit her, you say. What about her ex-husband? He do it, too?"

"Never saw Jerry lay a hand on her, only Lee. But she apparently read him the riot act because he stopped doing it."

"You've been very helpful, sir," Gleason said, taking Lee Meadow's photo out of his coat pocket. "Just to make certain we're talking about the same individual, is this Lee Meadow?"

"That his booking picture?" Young said, eyeing the picture. "Looks like it ought to be. Yeah, that's the jerk. Got a bad temper, too, by the way."

"Thank you, sir," Gleason said, replacing the photo and handing him a card. "Please call if there's anything else you remember."

"About that accident," Young said. "Was Lee hurt?"

"He's in the hospital," Gleason said.

Powers was waiting for him in the car.

"How'd the sex talk go, sir?" she asked.

"Seems Mr. Young is a voyeur. Apparently, he's been watching the show next door for some time, too."

"Whips and chains?"

"Tame stuff, actually. Woman gets tied up. Young said her ex-husband used to do it before Meadow came on the scene."

"So, a little exhibitionism, too."

"Yeah, but Meadow got creative. Slapped her around a few times, apparently when he shouldn't have."

"That's a no-no," Powers said. "Without consent, it's assault. I'm a little familiar with the B.D.S.M. community."

Gleason paid her a curious look.

"Bondage, discipline, dominance, submission and sadomasochism. Gray area about legality. Some states have laws against it. Others turn a blind eye. All depends. The big thing they stress is it be safe, sane and consensual. And to know and set your limits. My guess would be that Lee Meadow didn't respect boundaries. He may not have been a real practitioner. Probably was a vanilla guy. That's what they call people outside of the community."

"I have to ask, Rachel," Gleason said. "Have you ever...or do you?"

"Never appealed to me but for the people it does, they take it seriously. And if you're not one of them, it's hard for an outsider to understand. It's just the way they're made. Live for extreme kicks. They get a rush. Sometimes just seeing what they can take. Doesn't mean they're always turned on either. When I was on active duty, we had a case involving a strangulation. Two consenting individuals but that doesn't mean you can legally do anything you want. In this instance, a person died. The victim's partner was convicted of involuntary manslaughter. Not a nice thing."

"Makes me wonder about our boy in the morgue," Gleason said. "Maybe he took the game too far with someone and it bit him."

"I'm not sure it'd go that way, sir. He'd just be dropped from the community. There are a number of good books on the subject, if you're interested."

"Well, we've got four more phone calls to check out," Gleason said, ignoring her last sentence. "See where they take us. By the way, I'm sorry if I got out of line with you back there."

"No problem, sir. How's the running going?"

"Thinking about doing the Seven Mile Bridge race."

Chapter 8

Jack had watched Rachel return to the car. He'd decided not to bother her and remained inside his house. Five minutes later, Gleason showed up and they drove away. He wondered what they'd discovered, if anything.

He walked down to the neighbor's house. Victor Young was puttering around in his front yard.

"Terrible thing about Lee Meadow," Jack said.

"Doesn't surprise me. He drives like a maniac."

Jack frowned.

"Don't see how that has anything to do with it," he said.

"Accident waiting to happen, if you ask me," Young said. "Hope no one else was hurt. Guy probably doesn't even have insurance."

"Are we talking about the same thing?" Jack asked.

"Couple of detectives were just here investigating," Young said. "Talked at length with me. First, I thought it had to with Candace but it turns out they meant Lee. Seems he wrecked his damn truck. My guess is alcohol was involved. Or drugs."

"You see the paper this morning?" Jack asked.

"That rag?" Young scoffed. "I stopped subscribing to it months ago."

"Well, Lee Meadow's picture is in it. Didn't mention anything about an automobile accident. Only that his body was found on Truman Beach. That's why the detectives were here."

~~~

"I could stay another night," Amanda said dreamily.

"We can do that," Drake smiled. "Haven't checked out yet. You up for it, Candace?"

The three of them were having brunch on the patio at a small luxury hotel in Coconut Grove.

"Not sure I'm very good company right now," Candace pouted. "Maybe it'd be better if I went home."

"Oh, sweetie, you're the best of company," Amanda cooed. "We love you. Tell her so, Drake."

"There are some terrific places in South Beach," he said. "We can go clubbing."

"I can't seem to get out of this funk," Candace said. "It's driving me crazy."

"If you're having second thoughts about Lee, forget them," Amanda said. "Good riddance is all I can say."

"Okay, fine," Candace said, tossing Drake a quick glance. "We'll stay another night."

"That's our girl," Amanda said.

~~~

"You say your neighbor was the fellow you saw from the jet plane, Jack?"

Jack was at the Inedible Cafe, killing time until the plumber showed up at his house. The man had said he could still do the job today but it would be late before he could get to him.

"Longshore drift could've put the body right there where they found it," Billy offered.

"Longshore drift, you say. What's that?"

"Easy thing to understand, Jack. Drowned man sort of waltzes with the waves until they wash him up somewhere. Unless the fish eat him first. That big storm took him off that little key and put him on the beach where he was headed in the first place."

"You'd have thought someone would have spotted him along the way," Jack said. "Lot of boats out there."

"Dead man's not the easiest thing to see in the water. Sometimes he bobs along just beneath the surface until he makes his appearance, hee, hee. Speaking of bobs, what happened with Bobby Sunshine fixing that leak?"

Jack took a sip of wine.

"Bobby's no plumber. After a couple beers he admitted that his dad was a pipe-fitter and kept up their boat."

"So his dad just made it look easy. What do you think of that chardonnay?"

Billy had asked Jack to taste a new wine he was considering for the restaurant.

"California wine. From out in your old neighborhood, Jack. Place called Edna Valley. I ordered a few cases."

"Not sure I know where Edna Valley is, Billy, but this tastes pretty good. Maybe Derrick would like it for Stella by Starlight?"

"Derrick can pick his own damn wine. Doesn't need no help from me."

Uh-oh, Jack thought.

"What's up between you two?" he asked.

Derrick Bean was the chef at their other restaurant, Stella by Starlight, and ran the place pretty much on his own.

"We couldn't come to an understanding is all, hee, hee."

"Sounds like something Bobby Sunshine would say," Jack laughed.

Billy poured some wine into his glass and took a sip.

"Remember when Derrick had just hit town and I was showing him the ropes? Told him where to buy his fish and all. Important thing to know if you're running a seafood restaurant. But he decided to go with somebody else. Made me feel like a fool."

"As I recall, he did hire your buddy but the guy got arrested for bringing in illegals," Jack said. "Coast Guard took away his boat."

"Well, that's just it, Jack. He got that boat back last week. Told Derrick the fellow was good to go again. Derrick said he'd rather stick with the one he has. Made me look like a fool twice!"

Jack smiled.

"No reason to get your nose out of joint, Billy. I know for a fact that Derrick appreciates your helping him and respects your advice. Maybe you could place a couple of orders from your friend for here."

"Man I got now knows what he's doing. Make me a fool for the third time to cut him loose, hee, hee."

Billy finished his glass of wine.

"But you're right about the other thing, Jack. Derrick ought to have this chardonnay. I'll let him know."

~~~

Gleason and Powers had finished following up on the phone calls and were now back at the police station.

"So how does Key West rank on the face forgetfulness scale?" Gleason asked.

"Maybe close to the national average, sir."

"A couple of people were kind of vague," Gleason said. "Might've seen him."

"As in the face was familiar but they couldn't place the name?" Powers quipped. "I'm surprised we did as well as we did, sir. Like you said, Key West can be close- mouthed at times. Faces lost in the crowd."

"I found that contractor's take on him interesting," Gleason said. "Meadow was a good worker but mainly an asshole. They're doing a lot of rebuilding up by Marathon and he knows him from those. You want a coffee? I'll get it."

Gleason went to the coffee maker and returned with a couple of cups.

"There's another thing I was just thinking about," Powers said. "Victor Young told us that Lee Meadow kept a lot of junk in the backyard. I don't remember seeing any. In fact, the yard looked well-kept. Nothing lying around."

"Could be he cleaned it up," Gleason said. "Had a yard sale."

"If so, that sounds like he was planning to move. I wouldn't mind talking with Mr. Young again, sir."

The detective handling auto thefts called from across the room.

"Hey, Earl, the report on that truck you're looking for just came in from the Sheriffs."

Chapter 9

The two juveniles had been stopped for speeding on US1 just outside of Marathon. They couldn't produce a driver's license between them, nor a vehicle registration card for the truck, although they'd both sworn that it belonged to one or the other's uncle and he was okay with them using it. The truck was towed to the impound yard and the boys given a thrill ride in the cruiser to the Sheriff's station. Their parents were notified and once they'd arrived, the truth was tearfully exposed.

"Serial joyriders," the deputy said dryly.

Gleason and Powers were on the speaker phone with the Marathon Sheriff's substation.

"I'm familiar with that charge," Gleason chuckled.

"Kids noticed the truck parked on the street hadn't moved for a while," the deputy explained. "Checked it out and saw the keys were in the ignition. Decided to take it for a spin and made it back in one piece. Did the same thing next day. And the one after that. Fun, fun, fun until they got stopped."

"So what's next for them?" Gleason asked, dabbing at his nose with a tissue.

"Well, it's grand theft auto no matter how you look at it, detective, so they're facing a felony. But my guess is that'll be knocked down to a misdemeanor. Given their age and all. Probably be turned over to the city attorney, who'll talk with the kids and their parents. Doubt if it'll go to juvie court. Just put a good scare in them. Assign some after-school community work. If that doesn't set 'em on the straight and narrow, though, we'll be seeing them again."

Gleason and Powers nodded in agreement.

"The truck's in your impound yard?" Powers asked.

"That's right," the deputy said. "Since the owner apparently no longer needs it, I imagine someone in his family would want to bail it out."

"We're trying to run down the family," Powers said, "but before it's released to anyone, I'd like to have a print tech go over the interior. Also, could you find out from those two boys when they first noticed the truck? It'd be a big help to us and maybe help them by cooperating, you know?"

Powers thanked the deputy and they ended the call.

"Why do you want to dust it for prints?" Gleason asked.

"Nothing makes sense, sir. What was the truck doing in Marathon? Did Lee Meadow move there? We know he had work up there. But why were the keys left in the ignition? Like asking to be stolen. And another thing, where is this Farrow woman?"

~~~

"Well, you're all set to go, Mr. Hunter," the plumber said. "You're back in hot water now."

He laughed at his joke.

"What's the damage?" Jack asked.

"Since you'd already bought a new faucet set, it's just labor. Let's see, I was here for how long...oh, call it forty bucks?"

"Sold!" Jack grinned. "By the way, I like your company name."

"The Key West Plunger?" the man said. "It was my partner's idea."

Jack fished out two twenties and a ten from his billfold.

"That's for fitting me in," he said.

The plumber thanked him and left. Jack next texted Rachel Powers a message.

We have hot water.

Chapter 10

Jack slowly described a circle with his fingertips on the stomach of the woman lying beside him. Her skin felt smooth and cool from dampness. Silky and sleek.

All the covers were kicked to the foot of the bed.

She purred something and he raised up on his elbow.

"Isn't this when we're supposed to share a cigarette?" she asked, turning and pressing her body against him. "Like they did in the old movies, remember?"

"I've recently quit smoking again," he said, draping his arm over her waist. "But I can't think of a better reason to start."

"No, I wouldn't want to corrupt you."

"Too late."

"Besides, I think it's a nasty habit. What time is it?"

Rachel Powers pushed herself up to see the clock on the bedside table.

"I have to get up," she said.

"Why don't you stay the night?" Jack asked. "There's not much of it left anyway."

She wriggled back against the pillows and sat upright.

"I really can't," she said. "I didn't bring a change and I have an early call tomorrow."

"You could keep some clothes here," he said, testing the waters. "Wouldn't be any problem."

"Yes, that would certainly be convenient," she said, "but right now a lot is going on. I'd rather keep things the way they are for the time being. Is that all right?"

"Of course it is, Rachel. Look, I'm not trying to rush you into anything. Just want you to know that you've become important to me, that's all."

She turned her head to his and kissed him.

"I'd much rather share that lovely thought with you than any cigarette," she said and jumped out of bed to get dressed.

~~~

Gleason had been surprised to find Jay Halderman already in his office when he'd arrived at the police station. He'd figured *he* would have been the early bird this morning. Halderman motioned for him to come in.

"Good morning, Earl," the lieutenant greeted. "Have a seat."

"What did you do, Jay, spend the night?"

"Would've saved me having to dress for work," Halderman laughed. "How was your run this morning?"

"Didn't go. Came down with a damn cold."

"Summer cold's the devil to get rid of," Halderman said. "If you need any sick leave, don't be afraid to take it."

"Thanks," Gleason said. "It's just a minor annoyance. So what's up?"

"Wondering if you'd given any more thought to the lieutenants exam?"

Gleason gave a little laugh.

"To tell you the truth, we've been so busy I'd forgotten all about it," he said. "Besides, there's enough brass around here without adding another hat."

Halderman smiled.

"That's one way of looking at it," he said. "How many years have you been with the department, Earl? Don't answer. I can tell you. Fifteen, right? Ten of them in detectives."

"Yeah ..." Gleason answered slowly. "And ...?"

"So, all things considered, you're looking at another ten or fifteen until retirement, right?"

"Little early to be thinking about that, lieutenant. Retirement's not exactly on the horizon at the moment."

Actually, the subject had crossed his mind recently. But then it'd also raised a question. What else would he do? Head up security at a shopping mall?

"I have a silver anniversary coming up next year," Halderman said. "Married to this place for twenty-five years. So retirement's well in view on my particular horizon."

Gleason wondered if he should say congratulations but decided to keep his mouth shut.

"Earl, I'd like you to consider taking over when the time comes. You're the most qualified. What do you say?"

Gleason folded his arms.

"Do I have to answer now?" he asked.

"No, but you should give it serious thought. I believe you'd be the right man for the job. Meanwhile, take the lieutenants exam. You can always refuse the promotion."

Gleason got up to leave.

"Watch that cold, Earl. Remember, take some time off if you need."

"Got it under control," Gleason said.

"And don't forget what we talked about," Halderman called after him.

Powers had just arrived and was making herself a cup of coffee in the break area when Gleason joined her.

"Good morning, sir. You're here early."

"Should've stayed in bed," he grumbled good-naturedly.

"Sir?"

"Got out of bed on the wrong side. How was your night?"

Powers smiled, thinking she'd recently gotten out of bed herself. And definitely on a better side.

"Slept like a baby, sir."

They carried the coffees back to the detective's room.

"Wonder if the ME has scheduled the Meadow autopsy," Gleason said, pulling out a tissue from the box on his desk. "Better see what's up with him."

"I'd like to talk with Victor Young again," Powers said. "Curious about that backyard at the Meadow house. What happened to all the junk that was supposed to be in it?"

"Let's give 'em both a call. Get this show on the road."

~~~

After Rachel had left Jack, he'd gone back to bed. But sleep being ever evasive, he'd grown tired of playing its game and had gotten up and dressed.

He kicked around the house for awhile and finally, with nothing else to do, decided to take a walk. It was still dark.

Duval Street had been dead save for a few last spasms of nightlife somewhere farther down. He crossed over and cut up to Truman. The late night air held an unseasonal chill and he bunched his shoulders, stuffed his hands in his pockets and picked up his pace.

Morning traffic was already underway along Truman Avenue. Jack turned off at Margaret Street, preferring the quieter residential neighborhood. Up ahead a car had stopped to let someone out and then had driven off.

Jack saw that it was a woman, apparently a nurse judging by what she was wearing. He figured she was just coming off duty. She stood on the sidewalk fumbling in her purse. Her uniform seemed to be more of a costume. The dress was skintight, short and revealing. A hat perched on her head was almost comical with a huge red cross on its front. She found her house key and gave Jack a dirty look as he passed by.

He continued – moving like a chess piece – through, over and along the short streets until he'd come to Dog Beach. There, he found a piece of driftwood on the tiny strip of sand and sat down, the sun rising out of the Florida Straits warming his face.

His thoughts turned to his relationship with Rachel Powers. And how it'd begun. Apparently unnoticed by either one of them until it was too late and they were hopelessly ensnared. But wasn't that always the way it worked?

Certainly, the attraction had always been there, although he had been slow to recognize it. He'd at first thought she was only interested in arresting him on suspicion of murder. Fortunately, the real killer had been caught. But during the investigation, he'd started feeling something magnetic. And now they were an item.

The sun had climbed farther into the day when his stomach reminded him that it'd been some time since he had last eaten. Louie's Backyard wasn't open yet, but the Casa Marina Hotel was just up the street. He got up from his makeshift bench and headed there.

Chapter 11

Drake Boynton pulled the Lexus into the driveway.

"Wake up, kids," he said. "We're home."

"Thank God for small favors," Amanda muttered sleepily. "C'mon, Candace, sit up straight. You're crushing me.'"

Candace had fallen asleep leaning against her. They'd both ridden in the back seat down from Miami.

"What!" she said, startled, then rubbed her eyes. "I was having such a bad dream. Why'd we have to leave Miami so early anyway?"

"Only way to beat the traffic," Drake told her. "Otherwise you'd be bitching about how long it was taking."

"You can have a nap here, honey, before you go home," Amanda said. "Think I will, too."

"Tell you what, girls," Drake said. "I'm going to the airport after everyone's settled. Why don't we all meet at Louie's for lunch? Good idea?"

Amanda looked at her watch.

"Can we make it a late lunch?"

"They always turn out that way," Drake laughed.

~~~

Gleason and Powers decided that there was no need for both of them to see Victor Young again. And while Gleason had established a kind of rapport with him – meaning man-talk – Powers could approach him from a different angle. Neither detective could say exactly what that might be, however.

She drove past Jack's house and parked in front of Candace Farrow's on the chance that she might be home. Several knocks on the door determined no one was there. Or else they weren't answering. She stuck a business card in the door jamb and went next door. Victor Young answered on the first ring.

"Good morning, sir," she said. "I'm Detective Rachel Powers. You spoke with my partner and myself earlier."

43

Young stepped out on the porch.

"Why didn't you say he'd drowned?" he demanded. "Didn't find out what'd really happened until my neighbor told me."

"I'm sorry about that, sir. I now realize you believed at first we were investigating an automobile accident. I thought my partner had made it clear that it was a drowning after I'd left. Apparently he didn't. Or perhaps he just didn't want to needlessly upset you. He can be like that at times. Can't say if it's to his credit or not."

Powers smiled, mentally crossing her fingers, in hope the excuse would work. It was the best she could come up with at the moment.

"Sensitive type, huh? Didn't strike me that way but I guess it takes all kinds. Suppose that helps in your business – good cop, bad cop?"

Powers nodded.

"I just had a couple of follow-up questions," she said. "You mentioned that there was always a lot of junk in the backyard. We didn't see any. Do you know what happened to it?"

"Couple of men came and hauled it away. Probably took it to the dump."

"When was that?"

"I can't say exactly," he said, then petulantly added. "Not like I watch every damn thing that goes on over there, you know."

"Or course, sir. Would you say it was before or after you'd noticed Mr. Meadow's truck was missing?"

"Had to be afterwards. I thought Candace had kicked his butt out and he was having the junk taken to wherever he'd moved."

Powers paused for a moment.

"I know that they toyed in bondage," she said. "But were there other times ... when things got rougher?"

Young blushed.

"I've seen it all and heard it all, sir," Powers assured him. "Don't worry about embarrassing me."

"I saw him get physical with her a couple of times. I thought it was just part of their fun and games, you know.

44

They argued a lot. Rather he did. But after a while, Candace would just ignore him. Look, please understand. I don't eavesdrop but things like that you can't help but hear."

"Believe me, sir, I know how that can be," she said. "Lived in a few thin-walled apartments myself. What I could tell you about some of *my* former neighbors."

Young seemed a little more at ease.

"If Candace had...kicked his butt out...you have any idea where he might've landed?" Powers asked. "Could he have had any family, say, farther up the Keys like maybe Marathon?"

Young shook his head.

"No idea about any family," he said, "but contractors are begging for help with all the building still going on up the Keys. He could have moved for the work. Rent has to be cheaper there than in Key West."

"One more thing, sir. What about their friends? Ever have people over? Social stuff?"

"Candace and Jerry sometimes did," Young said. "That's her ex-husband, Jerry Holtz. Told your partner that. Used to be another couple that'd drop by regularly. Haven't seen them for a while."

"You ever meet them?"

"I wasn't really in their circle, if you know what I mean. We were just neighbors."

"How about the ex-husband? I believe you said Jerry Holtz? Is he still in Key West?"

"I'm not sure. Jerry sold boats. Some kind of marine broker. Think he might've gone up to Miami after the divorce."

Boats. That was huge, Powers thought.

"Again, you've been very helpful, Mr. Young."

She handed him her card.

"And I'm sorry about the little misunderstanding concerning Mr. Meadow," she added.

Leaving, she considered stopping by Jack's but continued on back to the police station. She'd give him a ring later. Also, she wanted to get back to Gleason about Jerry Holtz.

Chapter 12

Drake parked the Range Rover on the ramp and entered the hangar through its front door. He switched on the overhead lights and locked the door behind him to bar any unwanted visitors.

The building could accommodate two airplanes but only the little biplane was in there.

He stepped up on the bottom wing and carefully examined the new front-cockpit windscreen. This was the first chance he'd had since it'd been replaced. He would've preferred to have done the work himself. The only problem with that was he would've had to order a new windscreen from the factory. And they might have asked questions. How was it broken? During flight? Bird strike? They'd might even demand one of their engineers come out and have a look. The FAA might have become involved. Was there a design flaw? Should they issue an airworthiness directive? Why invite trouble?

Then there were the Federal regulations he would have run afoul of. While there were certain kinds of maintenance an aircraft owner was allowed to perform, replacing a windscreen was not one of them. That type of job required the service of a certified aviation mechanic.

At first, he'd considered having the work done at another airport. Perhaps even one in another state. But he decided that would only complicate things and possibly raise more questions.

Naturally, the nosy local mechanic he'd used wanted to know how it'd happened. With a sad shake of his head, he had explained it'd been an accident – a passenger had grabbed hold of the windscreen getting into the front seat and had put all his weight on it. The mechanic had then replied – with a sympathetic shake of *his* head – that the guy must've been a gorilla because the mounting brackets were damaged as well. They'd both agreed it was a shame.

47

So the official word – and entered in the aircraft maintenance log – was that the windscreen had been accidentally broken while the airplane was on the ground. No aerodynamics or inflight menaces involved. And no big deal other than a hefty repair bill which included the promise never to mention the incident. The mechanic had left the old broken windscreen on the work bench, as had been requested. Drake stuffed it into a large plastic trash bag and left, taking it with him.

And now the bag was hidden from sight behind the rear seat of the Range Rover as he drove to meet up with the girls at Louie's Backyard. He'd get rid of the thing later.

~~~

Jack had finished a leisurely breakfast complete with the *New York Times* and *Wall Street Journal*. He left the hotel and walked down Seminole Avenue before cutting over to Waddell and on to Vernon, which put him in front of Louie's Backyard. It was turning out to be another fine day and the moment couldn't have been more enticing to stop off for a drink on the deck.

He stood in the entrance way. The bar was full. However, there were a few empty chairs along the rail next to the water's edge. He started to go over when he noticed two women seated at a table. He recognized one of them. His neighbor, Candace Farrow.

Should he say something? Express his condolences? Tell her the police had dropped by while she was out? It was awkward.

"Excuse me," a man said behind him.

"Sorry," Jack apologized, realizing he was blocking the entrance and stepping out of the way.

The man nodded a thank-you and went directly to the table where Candace and her friend sat. He bent and kissed both of them before taking his seat.

This was very interesting, Jack thought. Candace didn't appear to be the grieving lover or whatever her relationship with Lee Meadow had been. But then he hadn't seen her in the neighborhood lately, had he? Perhaps she'd been out of town and had just arrived back home today. Didn't even know the guy was dead. It was possible.

He walked over to their table.

"Hi, Candace. I'm Jack Hunter. I live a couple houses down from you. Nice to see you."

She gave him a startled look but quickly collected herself.

"Sure," she said. "I remember you from the block party."

"Yeah, I talked with you and your friend that night," Jack said, then joked to the others, "I'd just moved into the neighborhood, but the party wasn't really for me."

Drake and Amanda smiled. Candace didn't introduce them to Jack. He wondered again if he should mention Lee. An uncomfortable silence began to form.

"I'd ask you to join us," she said quickly under a faint smile, "but I've been away for a while and we have some catching up to do. Please excuse me."

"Of course," Jack said. "I recently got back in town myself. Saw you sitting here and just thought I'd say hello. Have a good day."

At the deck's entrance he stopped to look back at the table. Candace's eyes were fixed on him.

"What do you know about him?" Drake asked, giving Jack a once-over himself.

"Nothing. Just that he's a neighbor."

"Funny, I picked up a strange vibe while he was here. He didn't say anything about Lee, either."

"I didn't like him at all," Amanda said. "I think we should leave. Now."

Jack gave them a little wave and continued on to the street.

~~~

Powers had returned to the police station and was talking with Gleason.

"The ex-husband's name is Jerry Holtz," she said excitedly. "And get this. He sells boats."

Gleason dabbed at his nose with a tissue.

"Yeah?"

"Possible motive and method right there. Let's say Holtz blamed Lee Meadow for breaking up his marriage. Somehow

49

he got him on a boat. I don't know, to talk things over. Make peace or have it out, whatever. Anyway, Meadow wound up in the ocean. Love and hate, most popular reasons for killing someone."

Gleason considered her premise.

"That could work," he said. "Where does the ex-hubby live?"

"I don't know. Victor Young said he thought he might be in Miami. Another thing, I think we should run him. Maybe he's a hothead and has a record."

"Ah, hold on for a minute," Gleason said. "We don't have any reason to run him. The only thing we know is he's the ex-husband. That's not a crime, yet. You know better than that."

Powers blushed.

"I do know better, sir. I've let myself get ahead of things here. It was just the news about the boat "

Powers had always been willing to stick her neck out if it was important. Time for her to put the brakes on.

"Happens now and then," Gleason said. "That's why it's against the law for us to look into a citizen's business unless we have reason. Still no joy on the Farrow woman, huh?"

"Left a card in her door."

"All we can do for now. The medical examiners' office said they hope to get to Mr. Meadow tomorrow or the next day at the most. Want to be there?"

"An offer I can't turn down."

"I'll get us a couple of tickets."

Power's cellphone chimed with a text message. She saw it was from Jack.

I'm in front of Louie's Backyard. Candace Farrow is sitting on the deck.

Chapter 13

Gleason saw Jack waiting by the bicycle rack in front of Dog Beach as he and Powers pulled up.

"I'll park there," he said, nodding to where Jack stood.

Powers had phoned Jack immediately after receiving his text message. He'd explained that he had not brought up what'd happened to Lee Meadow, only that he'd referred to him as her friend when he'd met at the block party. He said he'd wait until they'd arrived in case Candace left.

"Remember, we just want to inform the woman of Lee Meadow's death," Gleason reminded, "not cuff her."

Powers replied with a roll of her eyes.

"No one's come out," Jack said when Gleason opened the car door.

"Okay, show us where they're sitting," he said, "and then keep out of the way."

Jack led them back to the deck.

"They're gone!" he said, stopping at the entrance and staring at the empty table. He quickly went over to the outside bar, Gleason and Powers following.

"Do you remember the people sitting over there?" he asked the barkeeper. "Two women and a man. They were just here ten or fifteen minutes ago."

The bartender looked to where he was pointing.

"No, but I've been pretty busy," he said and then asked the waitperson who'd come up. "Val, you serve the people at that table?"

"They left before I could take their order," she said.

"That's impossible!" Jack argued. "I was out front the whole time. They couldn't have left without me seeing them."

"Oh, they went next door," Val smiled, motioning to the hotel adjoining the deck. "There's an entrance on the other side of the bar. Is there some kind of problem?"

"No, ma'am," Gleason said. "Just trying to locate someone."

51

He and Powers turned to leave.

"Wait a minute," Jack said. "Aren't you going to check that hotel?"

"Who do I ask for?" Gleason shrugged.

~~~

Candace had picked up her car at the Boyntons and was driving to her house. She still felt a little unnerved. The chance meeting with Jack had been a surprise but nothing more. Until Drake had mentioned his strange vibes and Amanda had been spooked so much she insisted they immediately leave. Escape was more like it, the way she'd acted. Having to cut through that hotel and hide there while Drake went to get the car. Really! By the time they'd reached home, though, all three of them were bordering on hysterics.

Well, what else would you expect? They were besties, weren't they. Totally wired on the same circuit, they liked to say of themselves. She gave a little laugh and parked. Home sweet home, she thought ironically getting out. She hadn't noticed Victor Young squatting by some sickly plant he was fussing over.

"Hi, Candace," he said somberly. "Terrible thing about Lee. If you need anything, let me know."

"I'm sorry?"

"At first, I thought he'd moved," Victor said, getting to his feet and walking over to her. "Hadn't seen his truck around and all. Looked to me like you two had split up. So when the police said they were investigating an accident, I jumped to conclusions about Lee's leaving and it being the reason the truck was gone. Thought he'd been in some kind of accident. Hate to say it, but I was kind of relieved it wasn't you that'd been injured."

"I don't understand what you're talking about," Candace interrupted. "The police were here about an accident?"

"Well, yes, they came by twice actually. Like I said, the first time..."

"What did they want?" Candace broke in. "What accident?"

"I'm trying to tell you," Victor said. "The first time they seemed interested in Lee but they never said that he'd drowned and that's why they were here. Just said they were investigating an accident. I had to find out what'd really happened from our neighbor."

"What neighbor?" Candace asked anxiously.

"Jack Hunter," he said, motioning toward Jack's house. "He showed me the newspaper article with Lee's picture, Made me feel kind of foolish, too, since I'd gone on about Lee being a bad driver and all. When that detective came back the second time, I let her know that I didn't appreciate their playing with me like that."

Candace momentarily shut her eyes as her thoughts raced back to Louie's. Jack Hunter exchanging pleasantries while knowing all the time about Lee. Why? What's his game? She really didn't know anything about him. And now Lee's picture was in the paper as a drowning victim? Yet the police are investigating? When she opened her eyes, any fear that might've been in them had been replaced by anger.

"Thank you, Victor," she said coolly.

Unlocking the front door, she saw a business card stuck in the frame. She put it in her purse and went inside.

~~~

"At least Jack was right," Powers said. "I'm certain he recognized Candace Farrow. Wonder where she's been?"

She and Gleason had returned to the station and were at their desk.

"I'm not doubting that your friend recognized her, Rachel, it just turned out to be a typical Hunter fiasco. Frankly, I've come to expect them."

"But that's his charm, don't you know?" she smiled. "Although, you have to admit he's been on the mark about first seeing the body *and* identifying it. Personally, as to his latest...fiasco...I think those people with her at Louie's had a sixth sense."

"Could be," Gleason said. "Still, we don't have anything one way or the other on Lee Meadow and won't until we get the autopsy results. And as far as the people she was with, there's nothing to connect them with anything. Sixth senses notwithstanding."

"What about the truck?" Powers asked, changing the subject. "Print report come in?"

"I'll call the Marathon Sheriffs."

"Here's another thought," Powers said. "Why don't we have the truck brought to the Sheriffs impound on Stock Island? No one's going to ask about it up there. It might help us to have it here."

"It's the Sheriffs' investigation up there, Rachael. Not sure they'll go along with that but I'll ask."

~~~

"Jack, I was just thinking of calling you, hee-hee," Billy said. "Found out something that might be a nice treat for you and your lady friend. Fellow who lives in the neighborhood told me about it. Name's Cosmo."

Jack had stopped by the Inedible Cafe on his way home from Louie's. Billy was in the back at the Undrinkable Bar wiping down the counter. Jack went behind the bar and pulled a beer out of the cooler.

"But before I get around to what Cosmo does, got something else to tell you," Billy said excitedly.

Jack popped the top off the bottle and took a seat at the bar.

"So tell me," he said.

"Found us a new bartender to fill in on weekend nights, "Billy said. "Name is Albena. Pretty name, huh?"

"Al who?"

"Albena. Knows when a drink's mixed right just by its weight, too. Ain't that something?"

"That doesn't make sense, Billy."

"True fact, Jack. Proved it right here at the bar. Mixed up several martinis. Every damn one came out perfect. No short pours. No spillovers. Takes time to learn how to do it, of course. Real professional."

"What's this person's name again?"

"Albena."

""Never heard of him. Don't see what's so pretty about the name either. Now, what's the other thing?"

"Something for when the wedding bells ring." Billy said. "That's where Cosmo fits in."

"Might be awhile before that happens," Jack smiled. "So what's his deal?"

"Cosmo makes dried rose pedals. Only thing is they don't look dry. Has a special way to treat the pedals so they stay fresh. Showed me a box full of them, Jack. Looked like they just fell off the rosebush."

"How do you know they didn't?"

"Fellow doubts everything misses out on half of life," Billy admonished. "You ever hear that?"

"Okay, what does he do with them?" Jack asked, taking a pull from his bottle.

"Does weddings, Jack. Sprinkles pedals up and down the church aisle for the happy couple's walk on the big day but he doesn't stop there, hee-hee. The other thing he does is the bedroom."

Billy paused for effect.

"Sprinkles those rose pedals all over the bedroom floor," he continued. "Then for a piece of resisting, he makes a heart out of them right in the middle of the bed."

Jack put his head down on the bar and laughed.

"Fellow's a romantic, Jack. Like you."

Chapter 14

"**H**omicide, Detective Powers. How may I help you?"
There was silence on the other end of the phone line followed by a hang-up.

Powers looked at her phone and shrugged.

"Who was that?" Gleason asked.

"Wrong number, I guess."

"Yeah, they were probably calling Sandy's Cafe for take-out," Gleason wisecracked. "Actually, that's happened before."

Powers smiled.

"Good idea, sir," she said. "I could do with a Cuban sandwich. Let's order."

"Kind of lost my appetite," Gleason said. "Can't seem to shake this cold."

"Why don't you take the rest of the day off? Hot shower and bed might help. I could check out Lee Meadow's truck since the Sheriffs were kind enough to put it in our yard."

"Don't know what you expect to find, Rachel. Only prints in it belonged to those kids. You read the report."

"Doesn't that seem odd, sir? I would've thought some of the owner's fingerprints would've been present."

"Yeah, but even if someone wiped it down where does that leave us? Could've been the truck was stolen in Key West and the thief was clever enough to clean up after dumping it."

"Exactly, sir."

Gleason thought that over.

"See what you can find, Rachel," he said. "I'll be at home. Call if you need anything."

~~~

Candace had recovered from the initial shock of learning that the police had been at her house and obviously wanted to talk with her. How had they even known Lee lived there? She doubted that he had sent out any change of address notices when he'd moved in. He kept a post office box.

She'd decided to take matters in hand and call the police. An offense is a good defense or whatever the hell it was that her ex-husband used to parrot. Besides, they'd get around to her sooner or later. She just hadn't expected a homicide detective to answer. She had better find out a little more about what was going on. Specifically, what did the police know?

Now she sat in the reading area of the Key West Library. A stack of newspapers on the table in front of her. Lee Meadow staring at her from out of one. Whatever answers she might been looking for, she wasn't going to find them here. There was nothing other than the victim now had a name. She left the pile of papers where they were.

~~~

"Dead battery, ma'am."

"I know that," Powers said exasperatedly. "Just jumpstart it and I'll get the thing charged later."

She was stuck in the department parking lot.

"That's iffy," the tow truck driver said. "Probably your alternator's not working. If that's so, then you're going to be left high and dry the next time."

"Then what do you suggest?"

"We jumpstart it and you drive to the garage and let the mechanic check out the electrics. Could be the battery's old and needs replacing. If the alternator's shot, he'll have to order a new one."

"I suppose you're right."

The engine fired up in a flash. While the man unhooked the starting cables, Powers wondered if she should chance it and drive out to the impound yard anyway.

"All set to go, ma'am," he said, slamming down the hood. "You can follow me if you like."

Powers thought for a couple of seconds before making up her mind.

"Okay, lead the way."

~~~

Jack saw Victor Young wave at him as he drove into the lane. He continued on down to him.

"What's going on, Victor? You okay?"

"Man, I love that Jeep," Victor grinned. "Gonna have to get me one someday. Anyway, wanted to say my neighbor's back."

"I saw Candace earlier," Jack said. "She was with some friends."

"Awfully sad, her not knowing about Lee and them having broken up."

"Not sure I'm following you, Victor."

"Same thing as happened to me, Jack. Remember I hadn't realized he'd drowned until I saw that newspaper story? Then, like a jerk, I did it with Candace. First thing I said to her is how sorry I was. Don't believe she knew he was dead until I told her."

That was the second time that possibility had cropped up. He'd considered it himself after talking with her at Louie's.

"Candace home now?" Jack asked.

"No, she took off a little while ago. Seemed a little upset to me. Can't say I blame her."

~~~

"Alternator's not putting out," the mechanic announced gravely. "Have to replace it. Don't know if the battery will hold a charge. It's pretty old. Personally, I'd go with a new one."

"When can I get my car back?" Powers asked, seeing only a big chunk of money sprouting wings and flying off.

"Tomorrow afternoon. Give me a call first."

"Is it possible you could do it sooner?" Powers asked. "I really need the car."

"Depends on when I get the new alternator. Has to come down from Miami. Be a special order, too, since it's for the big engine. I'll get on it soon as it comes. Best I can promise."

"Look, it's running now," she said. "Couldn't I take a chance and drive it?"

"You could but I wouldn't recommend that. No guarantee it'd start again if you turned off the ignition. Like I said, the alternator's not putting out enough juice and the battery's probably too weak to hold it anyway. You'd just be calling us again."

"All right," Powers nodded, "I'll leave it here. Oh, you wouldn't happen to have a loner car would you?"

"No, ma'am."

Well, that shot down any hope of going to the impound yard she thought to herself. She might as well take the rest of the day off. She took out her cellphone to call a taxi. Then she had another idea.

"Hi, Rachel," Jack said, recognizing the number and answering on the first ring. "You at work?"

"I've got a dead battery."

"Another homicide case, huh?"

"It's not funny, Jack. My car's in the shop and I need a favor."

"Sorry, couldn't resist. What can I do?"

Fifteen minutes later the red Jeep drove up.

"You'll have to show me the way," Jack said, as Powers climbed into the passenger seat.

"Thanks for coming," she said. "The impound yard's on Stock Island. Can you wait for me? I won't be long."

~~~

Long was a matter of perception, Jack realized as he sat in the Jeep parked to the side of the gate. She was taking forever. He hadn't been allowed to go inside with her since he had no business there. It wasn't his stolen vehicle that Powers wanted to examine, the man in charge had pointed out. He checked his watch again and peered through the chain-link fence.

Powers had found nothing new in the truck. She'd gone over it stem to stern, inside and out. The print tech had grabbed plenty of impressions in the cab, all belonging to the boys. Their prints were on the steering wheel, door handles and the glove compartment, which they'd obviously ransacked. That'd been covered in the tech report which she'd gotten earlier. It would seem that every surface had been swiped clean before the two boys ever set foot in the truck.

Why had someone gone to all that trouble? She couldn't imagine it being Lee Meadow with a handy-wipe, but who knows? Maybe he was obsessive-compulsive about germs. She didn't really believe an ordinary car thief would've been so careful about not leaving any prints behind. No, this was done for another reason. And the first one to come to mind is to prevent identification. Leaving the keys in the ignition was also purposely done, she'd bet. Make it a sitting duck for anyone passing by. But again, why? So far everything about this investigation had only raised questions.

She locked the truck and was walking back to the yard's office to return the truck's keys when she literally stopped in her tracks. She hadn't noticed until that moment the chain also held a set of house keys. Were they for a new address or an old one?

However, the truck was stolen property. The keys were evidence in an ongoing case. She would need a court order to take them. And a stronger reason than a fishing trip to get one.

Or she could just absentmindedly place them in her purse and walk out.

Chapter 15

Candace sat in her car at the corner of Margaret Street and Truman Avenue waiting for a break in the traffic so she could pull out and onto the main drag. The stoplight at Windsor Lane had cars lined up for two blocks beyond her. It was that time of day. Finally, the line started to move, then immediately stopped, a red Jeep easing in to the slot she was just about to take. She felt like blowing her horn and giving its inconsiderate occupants the finger. She studied the jerk behind the wheel and his girlfriend next to him blabbing away. The Jeep looked familiar. And now, come to think of it, so did the jerk. She didn't recognize the woman.

The cars started to move again. Eastbound traffic hadn't reached her yet. She quickly turned right onto Truman and stepped on it. Suddenly, for some reason, she didn't feel like going home.

~~~

"Are you sure you won't need it?" Powers asked.

"How many times do I have to say?" Jack laughed. "No, I won't need the Jeep and you can use it as long as you want. Okay?"

"That's awfully sweet of you. It's that I might have to be at the morgue sometime tomorrow. With any luck, though, my car could be ready then."

They'd just parked in front of Jack's house.

"You do know how to drive a stick shift?" he asked.

"Of course, I do," Powers said. "It's that thing on the floor, right? Push it forward to go ahead. Pull it back for reverse. How hard is that?"

"You've got it."

Powers turned to look down the street.

"I wonder if your neighbor is home," she said. "Would you mind waiting here? I'll only be a moment."

"Now, where have I heard that before?" Jack smiled. "Sure, go ahead. I'll be inside the house."

Did she really want to do this, Powers thought to herself as she walked to Candace's house. She was flying blind here and definitely stepping over the line, though in her mind it was just a baby step. Maybe the woman would be at home and none of this would be necessary.

She rang the doorbell, noticing that her card was missing from where she'd placed it. Getting no answer, she next peeked through the window to the front room and tapped on it. Nothing.

Back to the door, she gave the bell another try and waited. No answer. She should turn around right now and leave, she knew that.

She took the truck's keys from her purse. There were two locks on the door. Shielding herself as best she could from any passerby, she slipped one of the keys into the top lock. It didn't fit. She tried the other one. It easily slid into place. She tried the other key with the lower lock. Same results. No question that the keys were to Candace Farrow's house.

She hadn't opened the locks because she wasn't absolutely certain no one was home. They could've just not answered the door. They would've heard the latches and that might have caused other problems.

She now believed for certain that this was Lee Meadow's last address. Was learning that information worth jeopardizing her career? She hasn't come to that bridge yet. She looked around one last time and left for Jack's.

She hadn't seen Victor Young watching from his window next door.

~~~

"It was so unnerving," Candace explained. "First at Louie's and then there he is again, right in front of me. What are the odds for that? I think he's following me."

"I'm afraid you're letting your imagination run away with you, dear," Amanda said soothingly, placing a hand on her arm. "This is a small island, after all. I'm sure it was just a coincidence, don't you agree, Drake?"

The three of them were seated on the patio. Candace had driven to their home immediately after seeing Jack drive past.

"Has to be a coincidence, Candace," Drake said, refilling her wine glass. "What do you know about this Jack Hunter, other than him being your neighbor?"

"Nothing really. I met him that one time at the party, as I told you. But then I found out that he'd talked to the idiot who lives beside me about Lee. Even showed him the newspaper story. Why did he go out of his way to do that?"

Drake shrugged.

"Yeah, too bad you had to learn about Lee that way. Didn't know myself what'd happened since I haven't read the paper in days."

Candace cut her eyes at him. He smiled back.

"The thing is, he knew Lee was dead when he saw us at Louie's but never mentioned it," she said. "Don't you think that's a little strange?"

"Some people are like that," Drake said, brushing it off. "Avoid sensitive subjects. Afraid they might upset you."

"Drake's right," Amanda agreed. "I didn't care for the man but that doesn't mean he's up to something. Spend the night here with us. You can go home tomorrow when you're feeling better."

"But both of you said something was funny about him," Candace insisted. "That's why we left. Now he's just a busybody? You're all right with that? I'm not."

"Well, I guess it's true," Drake said. "Just because you're paranoid doesn't mean someone isn't following you. Tell you what. Let's order in. Chinese okay with everyone? I'll call the restaurant. Meanwhile, looks like we could use another bottle of wine. And later we can check out this Jack Hunter on the internet. Put this thing to rest."

Drake got up from the table and went inside.

"Excuse me," Candace said to Amanda. "I need to use the bathroom."

She caught up with Drake in the kitchen.

"What's that funny smell?" she asked. "Like shoes burning."

"You mean the candles? Amanda got them. It's called 'Leather'. I think it's quite nice."

"Look, I'm not sure you understand the significance of what's going on," Candace said. "First, my neighbor tells me he's sorry about what'd happened to Lee. Before I can take that in, he goes on to say Jack Hunter had told him because the cops hadn't mentioned anything about it to him during their chat when they'd dropped by the house. Cops? But he straightened them out on their second visit. A policewoman by herself this time. Why so many cops? She'd left her card and I called. Guess what? She's a homicide detective. I hung up without saying anything. Oh, and according to my nosey neighbor, Hunter's apparently friendly with the police. Maybe she's who I saw him with in his damn Jeep."

Drake opened a bottle of wine.

"I think this chardonnay will do nicely," he said, presenting the label to her.

Chapter 16

"**D**oesn't look good for the neighborhood with the police always snooping around," Victor Young said over the phone.

"Sir, they're just doing their job," Halderman said back.

"But they've been here three times, for Christ's sake." Young whined. "I mean, the man drowned. We're not talking about a mass shooting. It was an accident. What more do they need to know?"

"We try to be thorough, Mr. Young. I'll speak with the officers."

"Be sure to include the woman detective when you do. She was here again yesterday poking her nose in. Pushy, too. I don't want to have to call the mayor."

"I appreciate your concern, sir."

What a crank, Halderman thought, hanging up. He went to get a cup of coffee. Gleason had just arrived and had stopped at the machine before going to the detective's room.

"How's the cold, Earl?"

"Think I'm getting a handle on it. Had a good run this morning."

"Yeah? Well, don't overdo it. Say, I just got off the horn with Victor Young. Not a happy camper."

Gleason splashed some milk in his coffee.

"You want this before I put it back in the refrigerator?"

"Just a touch if you will," Halderman said.

"Victor Young," Gleason nodded. "He lives next door to the guy in the morgue, Lee Meadow. What did he want?"

"Has an issue with snooping," Halderman said. "Says you and Powers are giving the neighborhood a bad name by snooping around so much."

"Snooping, huh?" Gleason grinned. "Guess it takes one to know one. We ran into him the first time we went there. Right after Jack Hunter called in the ID on Meadow. Young came out of his house and wanted to know what we were doing. We

67

had a little chat. Got an interesting take on Meadow and the woman who owns the place. Young impressed me as being a busybody. Likes to peek in his neighbor's bedroom window, too. Rachel did a follow-up call on her own. That's about it."

"Mr. Young claims it was three times," Halderman said. "Threatened to call the mayor."

"Maybe he counted one of his fingers twice," Gleason shrugged.

"Seemed more upset with Powers. Did she say how the callback went?"

"Guess it was okay," Gleason said, "otherwise she'd have told me. She did get the ex-husband's name. Found out he was a yacht broker. Thought we might have something there. The guy no longer lived in Key West, had moved to Miami. Finally got in touch with him and it turned out he'd been in Europe at some big boat show for the past month. Never heard of Lee Meadow."

"Meadow was the woman's boyfriend, right?"

"Yeah, her name's' Candace Farrow. We're having a difficulty getting up with her. Our friend Jack Hunter spotted her at Louie's and called us but she'd gone when we got there. Could be Rachel then drove to the woman's house to see if she was home. Although the last thing she said to me was that she wanted to look at the truck in the impound yard."

"Well, I don't have a problem with any of this," Halderman said. "Just a heads-up about this Young character. Really don't need any heat from City Hall."

Gleason walked back to his desk to find Powers already seated at hers.

"Good morning, sir. How's the cold?"

"Lieutenant just asked me the same thing. I'm on the mend. Anything new on the truck?"

Powers considered whether she should tell him about the set of keys. She decided to hold off for the moment.

"Still puzzled over the only prints they could find belonged to the two kids," she said. "And the keys being conveniently left in it."

"Yeah, like it was asking to be stolen," Gleason agreed. "By the way, Victor Young phoned the LT this morning. All pissed off about the police snooping around so much at his neighbor's house. Mentioned you, in fact."

"Really? I don't understand why. As far as I was concerned, we had a good conversation. Speaking of facts, it was *you* that he was upset with. Said you'd led him on. I thought that was funny. But don't worry, I got you off the hook."

"You were over there yesterday?" Gleason asked.

Powers leaned back in her chair.

"Yes, I thought I'd check on Candace Farrow. No luck again."

"That's a long drive from the impound yard," Gleason said. "Any particular reason?"

She leaned forward, placing her elbows on the desktop and steepled her hands.

"Wishful thinking," she said, sweetly. "Any particular reason for your asking, sir?"

"Yeah, Young claimed we'd been there three times. Told the LT to my knowledge it'd been only twice. Just wanted to get it straight for the record."

She smiled.

"Well, for the record I *was* there yesterday. And to keep it straight, I didn't drive there myself from the impound yard. Jack Hunter drove me. My car broke down and he came to my rescue. He took me to the impound yard and then back to his house. He has even loaned me his Jeep until my car's repaired. Wasn't that nice of him? Anyway, since I was in the neighborhood, I thought I'd take the opportunity to look in on Miss Farrow. Unfortunately she wasn't home but I believe she had recently been there because my card was missing. Naturally, I left another one. Anything else, sir?"

Gleason started to protest but before he could reply his telephone rang.

"Detective Gleason, Blake Harding. I'm about ready to autopsy Lee Meadow. You and Detective Powers want to watch, get yourself in gear."

"We'll be there in about fifteen minutes, Doctor Harding," Gleason said and ended the call.

Powers gave him a sad smile.

"I didn't mean to tee off on you like that," she apologized.

"It's okay, Rachel, I was out of line questioning you. I think this case is getting to both of us."

"Sounds like what we need is a gory morning. Shall we go to the morgue?"

Chapter 17

"**H**e didn't drown," Blake Harding announced. "The blow behind his head is what killed him."

Lee Meadow's nude body was stretched out on the stainless-steel autopsy table. Harding turned the dead man's head to the side to show the injury. Powers bent down to take a picture of it. Gleason averted his eyes.

"That looked pretty bad to me when we found him at the beach," she said. "Wonder how it happened? We were thinking maybe he was knocked off a boat by the sail or something."

"It gets more interesting," Harding smiled. "He also fell from a great distance. Practically every organ in his body has been displaced. The aorta is torn. Liver ruptured. However, none of that would've mattered. He was dead before he hit the ground. Or in this case, I'm assuming the water's surface."

"How can that be?" Gleason asked.

"I can't imagine how he got himself in that situation," Harding said, "but I do know what the damage indicates. And that's sudden deceleration. See, it's not the speed that kills you, it's the stop."

"Could he have fallen off a cruise ship?" Powers asked. "Maybe he hit his head on the way down."

"I doubt that," Harding said. "For several reasons. But for the sake of argument, let's say it did happen the way you suggested."

"Those big ships are pretty tall," Powers said. "You have to admit."

"Yes, some a hundred feet tall, even more," Harding told her. "That could definitely kill you depending on how you hit the water. But let's go even taller. The Golden Gate Bridge in San Francisco, a suicide destination. At two-hundred and fifty feet from the railing to the water, few can people survive a drop like that."

"Even feet first?" Gleason interjected.

"Actually, the position doesn't really matter at that point," Harding answered.

"What about high divers?" Gleason persisted. "Like those guys in Mexico who jump off cliffs."

"They have to train for that so they don't hurt themselves," Harding said. "You have to hit the water just right and even then, if you're going too fast, you're out of luck. And if you belly flop off, you might as well have done it over concrete."

"So how fast do you think the victim was going?" Powers asked.

Harding did some mental calculating.

"Taking in the organ damage, I'd say he hit the surface at around a hundred and fifty miles an hour. See, a certain amount of water has to get out of the way when you enter. In a split second it has to move as fast as you're going. In this case, a hundred and fifty. Your body can't keep up with the forces involved."

"Yet he was already dead," Powers said. "I'm having trouble putting all this together."

"Let me explain a little more," Harding said. "You'll see why. It all has to do with physics. You've heard of the G factor? Airplane pilots talk about pulling Gs during maneuvers. That's a measurement of the force of gravity on a body in motion when it changes direction. You can feel it when you slam on the brakes in your car and you pull against the seat belt. Three or four Gs are okay. Starts getting uncomfortable when you go much higher. In a sudden deceleration, such as in a car crash at say, seventy miles an hour, you might experience forty Gs. Most people can just barely survive that. Now, what if you make that sudden stop from terminal velocity, that's the top speed a person reaches falling thought the atmosphere. Like our Mr. Meadow did. In the blink of an eye, everything in your body weighs seven thousand times as much. For example, your brain briefly weighs in at ten tons. No heavy-thinking jokes, please. And that brings us to the injury on the back of Mr. Meadow's head. That hole you can stick a finger in is where the ten-ton brain broke through a weak point in the cranium, one which could've only been made by an earlier blow to the head hard enough to indent the skull. It would've immediately been fatal. That portion of bone was blown out along with some brain matter at the moment of impact."

"What do you think he might've been hit with?" Powers asked.

"I don't know," Harding told her. "The shape of the hole is almost circular. Could've been a hammer. End of a pipe. Something round."

"Let me get this straight," Gleason said. "This guy hits the water going way over the speed limit. That he fell off a boat's out of the question. So it had to be an airplane, right?"

"The only thing I can think of," Harding said. "He had to have fallen several thousand feet to reach terminal velocity."

"Would that have torn off his clothes?" Powers asked. "He was completely nude on the beach."

"It's entirely possible," Harding said. "I once saw a guy dive off a high board at a pool and it tore off his swimming trunks. Didn't realize he'd lost them until he climbed out."

Harding gave a little chuckle at the memory.

"Back to the airplane," Gleason said. "Someone had to have tossed him out. That'd be more than a handful getting the body to the door. Also, you'd still have to fly the plane. So there must have been at least a couple of people involved."

"Don't planes have autopilots?" Powers asked. "Or is that only on big jets?"

"You'll have to ask a pilot about that," Harding said. "But here's something else that's interesting. I found a sliver of what seems to be plastic embedded in a wound on his forearm."

Harding displayed a small metal dish containing a clear shard.

"That should be marked as evidence," Gleason said. "Also, I'd like a photograph of it and where it was found on the victim."

"Yes, you definitely have a homicide now," Harding agreed. "I'll send this to the lab. Perhaps they can give us a rundown on its origin."

~~~

Gleason and Powers returned to the police station. Gleason stopped by Halderman's office to fill him in.

"Lee Meadow was dead before he hit the water," Gleason said. "The ME confirmed a blow to the back of his head killed him."

"Well, he probably would've died of fright anyway on the way down," Halderman said. "Had enough time to think about it."

"Dr. Harding says people don't usually die of fright in a fall."

"Then, I guess that makes it a dead drop for sure," Halderman laughed.

Gleason joined in the gallows humor. Sometimes it helped.

"We'll use that for the murder book title," he joked.

All homicide investigations begin with a ring binder notebook into which a record of every single piece of evidence is placed. It's an old-fashioned method of keeping track and so far nothing better has been invented. The Murder Book starts with the crime scene report, photos and the coroner's report. It always remains at the homicide table and is kept current until the case is closed.

"Detective Powers is getting one started," Gleason said.

"Oh, that reminds me," Halderman said. "Sheriffs impound yard called right after you left. Seems Powers didn't return some keys yesterday."

"I'll tell her to take them over. Not surprised that she was absent-minded. This whole Meadow business has been screwy from the start."

Powers looked up as Gleason approached.

"You have the keys to Lee Meadow's truck?" he asked. "Yard called the LT. Said they were missing."

Her stomach clenched. She hesitated a moment before answering.

"Funny, I thought I turned them in," she said with a puzzled expression.

She took her purse out from the desk drawer and rummaged through it.

"Here they are," she said, pulling out the keys. "Damn, I must have forgot."

Gleason frowned.

"You know the rules, Rachel. That's evidence. Especially now that this thing's turned into a homicide."

"Let's not go through that again, sir. You're right, of course, and I do understand."

"Just return them, okay?"

"I'll do that right now, if you don't mind. Shouldn't be take more than fifteen minutes. Be back in a jiffy."

There was no chance of sharing what she'd discovered about the house keys. She'd get her head handed to her. She'd have to keep that information to herself, at least for the time being. The maddening part was having to admit that he was right. Again. She'd never figured him for a follow-the-book guy. Still, he didn't have to be a prick. Maybe she should mess with his head a little.

"I was reading the coroner's report, sir," she said, gathering up her purse, "and a thought occurred to me. This could have been a suicide."

"Suicide? He was whacked in the head. You heard the doctor. You think Meadow did that to himself?"

"Suppose he simply hit his head on some debris? There's enough stuff floating in the ocean."

Gleason laughed.

"Okay, Rachel, I'll play along. The guy landed on a shipping container or whatever. How do you explain the airplane? Harding said he would've had to have fallen from more than a couple thousand feet."

"He could've taken a sightseeing ride in one," Powers said. "Easy enough to do right here in Key West. Or at the airport in Marathon. That'd explain why his truck was there. Anyway, when the time was right, he opened the door and jumped. The pilot was too frightened to report it. Or maybe the pilot was in on it. Been paid off. Assisted suicide. Wouldn't be the first time."

Gleason shook his head in amazement.

"It's not that far-fetched. sir," Powers persisted. "Dr. Harding said the Golden Gate bridge was a suicide destination. It's in the news a lot. We know things weren't going right between Lee Meadow and his girlfriend. Could've been depressed. Started having bad thoughts. Local airport's a lot closer than San Francisco. Just trying to look at it from another direction."

Gleason smirked.

"How about this? It was an accident. He was skydiving and hit his head on the door. Knocked him out, so he couldn't open the parachute. They were near the ocean and the wind somehow blew him over the water before he hit. Pilot never reported it because it'd be bad for business."

"There you go, sir. Another possibility. They're endless."

"Well, for now let's stick with homicide," he said.

Chapter 18

There'd been no problem returning the truck keys to the impound yard. Powers explained she must have absent-mindedly put them in her purse. She had been worried about keeping her friend waiting and had rushed out after examining the truck. She also informed them that the truck was now evidence in a homicide.

There had been a problem, however, when she stopped at the garage on her way back to check on her car. It wasn't ready. They'd had to order the alternator from another source. Something about the car being a special model. Big engine and all. Not that it made the car more valuable. Just more expensive to repair.

She'd then called Jack to ask if she could keep the Jeep. He'd been fine with that and said he could get around on Whizzer, explaining it was a bicycle he'd named it after a motorbike he once owned. She told him that she would like to hear the rest of the story but she was in a hurry to get back. It was getting late.

~~~

"A guy once jumped off the Seven Mile bridge," Gleason announced out of the blue. "It was the Sheriffs' case."

Powers had just walked in and hadn't even had a chance to sit down.

"The bridge is about eighty feet high where he stepped off." he continued. "Makes me wonder why Lee Meadow didn't bail off the bridge instead of taking flying lessons. It's convenient and a whole lot easier. Why, he could've even hit his head on something floating in the water under the bridge, as you suggested. That is, if your suicide theory is still on the table."

"I was just jerking your chain then, sir," Powers said, pulling out her chair. "Lee Meadow was murdered. The evidence is clear."

Which brings up the house keys again. Should she risk telling him what she'd found out? That they're the keys to the Farrow house. They could be evidence. Her acting without authority could make them inadmissible.

"Our mutual friend knew the jumper at the Seven Mile bridge," Gleason said.

"I'm sorry," she said. "My mind was elsewhere. Who did you say?"

"Jack Hunter. He'd been doing a quasi-investigation on the guy."

"That's incredible," Powers said. "What on earth for?"

"Had to do with some children buried in the cemetery. Hunter decided something was suspicious about their deaths and started nosing around. An old Key West family's name came up. He got in touch with the only two remaining members and evidently touched a nerve. Things got a little dicey for him. Nothing was ever proved."

"But apparently whatever he found out was enough to make one of them kill himself," Powers said. "How did Jack feel about that?"

"I think the whole thing hit him pretty hard," Gleason said. "He left town afterwards. Went back to Los Angeles."

"That's so sad. And there was nothing connecting the man to those children? The one who jumped off the bridge, I mean."

"No actual proof. Hunter even got me involved in helping him. Unofficially and off the record, of course."

"The two of you managed to work together? I'm surprised."

"Jack Hunter is a walking hurricane," Gleason said. "You learn to stay in the eye of the storm."

That might sound cute any other time, Powers thought, but at the moment, she wasn't in the mood for *cute*. She had a storm of her own making swirling around her. However, Gleason, whether by intention or not, had just given her a way out.

"Those keys I just returned?" she said. "There are a couple of others on the ring. They look like house keys."

No need to say anymore. Stay in the eye.

78

Gleason gave her a long look and flashed a wolfish grin. "Never know where a lead might turn up," he said.

"My thoughts exactly, sir."

Chapter 19

Candace lounged by the pool at the Boyntons. She'd spent most of the afternoon lazing there. The order-in dinner the night before had lasted much longer than anyone had expected, and they'd run through several bottles of wine during it.

"Are you awake?"

Amanda had come out to check on her friend.

"Drake has some news."

"What time is it?" Candace asked, sitting up and rubbing her eyes.

"Almost five."

"Christ, I should get home. What do you mean Drake has some news?"

"He found out about that dreadful man. Let's go inside."

Drake was in the library which also served as his office. He ran a small hedge fund from there.

"Lo, she lives," he joked at Candace's expense as the two women entered the room. "The sun's below the yardarm. I think that calls for a round of drinks."

"Ugh," Candace said, sticking out her tongue. "Don't think I'm ready for a drink."

"Oh, come on, honey," Amanda encouraged. "I'll go make a pitcher of bloody Marys. That okay with you, Drake?"

"Fine. Step over here, Candace. I want you to see this."

Drake stood aside so she could see the computer screen. "This your friend?"

Jack Hunter smiled at her. Only he looked different. He was dressed in a business suit and casually leaning against a desk. A large window behind him revealed the ocean.

"Cleans up good, huh? I hardly recognized him myself."

"Who is he?" Candace said. "I mean why's he there?"

"My question is why is he *here*?" Drake said. "This guy owns half of Los Angeles. Well, maybe not that much but what he does have is some pretty heavy real estate. And all of it is location, location, location. He's also a player in the stock market. Big time. Your neighbor is a very wealthy man."

"But he lives in that crummy little house," Candace said. "And why *is* he here? It doesn't make sense."

"Oh, but I think it does," Drake chuckled sarcastically. "Tell you why in a minute, but first, let's take a look at this character's background."

He clicked a couple of keys on the computer. A newspaper article popped up. Jack's picture was in it.

"You can find out anything about anyone these days," Drake said. "No secrets anymore. Everything's out there. Just have to know where to look. This story is from a few years back. Seems Jack Hunter was accused of murdering his wife in Los Angeles. Turned out he was innocent, and they eventually caught the real killer. Like that old saying goes, every cloud has a silver lining. However, Mr. Hunter's cloud had a gold lining. His deceased wife owned a large and successful real estate company in LA and he inherited the works. But here comes the interesting part. While the cops were looking for him in Los Angeles, he was on the lam, as they say, here in Key West."

"I still don't get it," Candace said.

"Fast forward," Drake chuckled again. "I said the man was a player in the stock market. In fact, he owns a considerable number of shares in a company we're presently targeting. Oddly, they're headquartered in Key West. Don't ask me why. Anyway, their board of directors have been reluctant to sell. I've managed to replace two seats but they still aren't listening to reason. And I think I know why. Jack Hunter has sided with them. His shares would give the holdouts controlling interest. That's why he's here."

"But what was all that about at Louie's? He knew Lee was dead and yet pretended nothing was wrong."

"Some crazy act he's playing is all I can say. I don't know why. Frankly, I think he was hoping you'd invite him to sit down so he could size me up. Yeah, he's keeping a low profile because of the stock deal. That would explain why he's living where he is instead of staying at a decent place."

Candace wasn't convinced. She decided to drop the subject, for now.

"You haven't said anything to Amanda...you know, about what happened?" she whispered, motioning toward the kitchen.

"Don't be silly. That between us. I don't want to bring her into this mess."

"Now, who's ready for a Bloody Mary?" Amanda chirped from the doorway.

~~~

Powers had just gotten home from work. She'd stripped down and was heading for the shower when the phone rang. The caller ID showed an out-of-state number.

"Detective Rachel Powers," she answered, slightly irritated at being interrupted. "Who is this?"

"Good afternoon, detective. This is Major John Goodman. I'm the Adjutant at Fort Benning CID. Hope I haven't caught you at a bad moment."

"No, sir," she answered, with a slight clearing of her throat. "Not at all. How can I help you?"

"First, I'd like to congratulate you on your promotion," the Major said.

"Thank you, sir. Didn't think the news travelled that far and broad."

"Depends on whom it concerns," Goodman joked. "In your case, it landed on my desk. I was just looking at your service record. Pretty commendable reading."

"Thank you again, sir. May I ask why you have it?"

"Absolutely. Your commanding officer recommended I review it. He thinks highly of you. He and I served together in Kaiserslautin. Actually, it was around the same time you were in Germany recovering at the hospital up in Landstuhl."

"That's all very interesting, sir, but what does this have to do with me?"

Goodman coughed a polite little laugh.

"Okay, I'll get straight to the point, detective. Have you given any further thought to what you and your CO discussed during your recent training exercises? I'm not trying to sound mysterious, but I can't go into detail over the phone. I can say you wouldn't be disappointed if you decide to go with it."

Powers paused.

"Sir, I have to be honest," she said. "I walked straight into a homicide investigation as soon as I got back. But yes, I have thought about it and I still am. I just haven't made up my mind. It's a big decision."

"Well, I can appreciate that. It *is* a big decision. I'm sure you're doing a fine job with the Key West police department and they wouldn't want to lose you. I guess one question to consider would be what's your next move there? In other words, where do you go from where you are now and will you be satisfied when you get there? Will it be enough?"

"Truthfully, I'm too busy to think about that, sir."

"That's a good answer. But that day *will* come. I can promise you this right now, the Army's wide open and will stay that way."

"I can't argue with that, sir."

"I don't mean to pry and please forgive me if I am, but I understand there's no family involved, is that right?"

"If you mean am I married, Major? The answer is no. I lost my husband in a helicopter accident. He was also Army. That probably wouldn't be in my service record. Nor should it. In fact, I've never mentioned it to anyone in my reserve unit."

"I didn't mean to offend you and I apologize. I was just wondering if there were someone you could talk this over with. Get another opinion. Again, I'm sorry to have intruded like that. It was rude of me."

"No, you were right. There is someone I need to talk with about this."

"Take as much time as you need. Of course, we'd like to hear from you sooner rather than later."

"You will, sir, and thank you for calling."

Chapter 20

Jack was bicycling along Petronia Street when he noticed a man posting a sign on a tree. The sign read, 'Help! Save Me!' He had to stop.

"Hey, what's with the sign?" Jack asked, sitting on his bike, one foot planted on the curb for balance.

"The city wants to take down the tree," the man told him. "Claims it's too messy."

The tree in question was an olive and the sidewalk beneath where it stood was indeed stained with fruit it'd dropped.

"Can't they keep the limbs trimmed back?" Jack asked. "Just the ones overhanging the walk?"

"More efficient to get rid of the whole thing. Only have to come out once for that."

Jack looked up at the tree.

"Seems like a shame," he said. "It's beautiful. Is it yours?"

"No, I don't live here. Owners out of town. Second home. I'm just trying to draw some attention to what's going on around town. They've already cut down a couple of mahogany trees. Butchered a healthy Spanish Lime over on Frances Street. What do they have against shade?"

Jack laughed.

"Well, good luck," he said. "What's your name?"

"I'm Chuck Banks."

"Glad to meet you, Chuck," Jack said. "I'm Jack Hunter."

"Watch out!" Chuck shouted, jumping back.

A car swerved toward them, its right-hand mirror clipping Jack's shoulder as it sped past. Both Jack and the bicycle went down.

"You okay?" Chuck asked worriedly, rushing over to help Jack.

"Yeah, I'm fine," Jack said, sitting a moment before getting to his feet. "Did you see who the hell that jerk was?"

"It all happened too fast. They didn't slow, either."

Jack rubbed at his shoulder.

"Don't think anything's broken," he said. "Probably be sore later."

"Maybe someone should look at that," Chuck said. "Want me to call 911?"

"No, I'm good."

He stood and bent down to pick up the bicycle. Its handlebars were twisted.

"Can't say the same for Whizzer."

Straddling the front wheel to hold the fork firm as he straightened the bars, a memory of the original Whizzer motorbike he'd once owned popped up. He had gone down on it after taking a curve too fast and had bent its handlebars to one side.

"Whizzer is what I call my bike," he explained. "Long story."

"Sure you don't want me to drive you to the hospital, Jack? My car's right across the street."

"Really, I'm all right."

"I think we should call the police," Chuck said.

"Wouldn't do any good. Neither one of us saw the car. Like you said, it happened too fast. Driver could've been drunk. Cops probably get two or three hit-and-runs like that every day."

"Yeah, lousy times we live in, huh?"

"Say, I believe I've seen you before," Jack smiled. "Where do you work?"

"I'm a waiter at La Trattoria on Duval."

"That's it. Now I remember. Took a couple of good friends there one night. You served our table. Well, thanks for everything, Chuck. Good luck with the trees."

Jack peddled away, a little wobbly, but the handlebars were straight.

~~~

Powers had decided a quiet drink in some place where she wouldn't run into anyone she knew would be a perfect setting to think things over. And where might that be? This was Key West, after all.

86

Yet there was such a place. The Naval Air Station Officers Club. She'd been there a couple of times and in both instances it was dead.

A short ride in the Jeep got her there and it was just as she'd hoped. Two men at the bar, apparently aviators since they had on their flying suits, and a man and woman in civilian clothes seated at a table.

She took a small table near the side of the room. The bartender walked over immediately.

"What can I get you, ma'am?" he asked with a slight Scottish burr.

"A gin and tonic, please. Light on the gin, if you will."

One of the men at the bar turned in her direction, then went back to his conversation with his friend. Another couple joined the one at the table. After a minute, they left together. The bartender returned with her drink.

"If that's too strong, let me know," he said. "Haven't seen you before, ma'am. You new at the base?"

"I'm Army."

"Well, we do get a few of them now and then," he laughed good-naturedly. "Anything else you need, give me a shout."

The last word came out as 'shoot'.

He left and she sipped her gin and tonic. It would do.

Now, about her situation. There was the present and the future. She hated the term 'pros and cons' but that was exactly what she had to consider. The good and bad, both professionally and personal. She wished she had a piece of paper so she could write them down. She mentally conjured up one.

She headed it *Present* and started with her job – homicide detective. On the *pro* side it offered interesting cases. She had a good solve rate. Great partner. She paused to think about Gleason. Yes, she decided, he was indeed that and also a good cop, even though he could be a pain when he wanted.

On the *con* side of her imaginary list, she wrote down small police department – that could also be a plus, but for now she'd keep it a minus. Limited room for advancement. Occasional interference from the brass.

She scratched out the last entry. It was unfair. Brass were everywhere.

Setting aside that list, she headed the next one *Personal*. It also began with *pro*. Key West was the first entry. Or did it belong on the other? She laughed to herself at that. No, she had nothing against the island. Although it was expensive to live here. And getting more so.

And then there was Jack Hunter.

They did have a relationship. She was happy with the way it was going. She also realized Jack wanted more. She wasn't blind. That would just have to be put on hold for the time being.

And finally, there was this. The Army was making her an extraordinary offer. What list did she put that on?

She mentally tore up the lists.

"Gentleman at the bar sends his compliments," the bartender said, placing a gin and tonic on the table. "He's also Army."

Powers looked. The aviators had been replaced by a man dressed in a light sport coat and slacks. He smiled. Her first reaction was to simply ignore him but for some inexplicable reason she smiled back. Right out of a corny movie, she thought. Next thing, he'll come over and ask to join me. She gave a silent groan.

"Thank him for me," she said.

She hadn't really wanted another drink. She'd just let it sit there. She saw her benefactor was now talking with the bartender. He wasn't bad looking. Kind of cute. Probably around her age, maybe a little older. She wondered what he did. He didn't impress her as being in some gung-ho outfit. To her surprise, he paid his bill and started to leave.

"Excuse me," she called out, as he headed toward the door.

He walked over to her.

"Yes, ma'am?"

"That was awfully nice of you to buy me the drink, but I think I'd rather have a cup of coffee. Would you care to join me?"

She couldn't believe what she'd just done. Maybe he'll say he has to be somewhere else. Important meeting. He's running late. Anything.

"I'd be delighted. Thank you."

He pulled out a chair and sat down. She noticed he appeared to be a little older than she'd thought but there was still a boyish charm about him. She liked that.

"The bartender said we worked for the same organization," he smiled. "I'm Mike Dana."

"I'm Rachel Powers."

"Here on vacation?"

"No, I live in Key West."

"Home on leave, huh?"

"No, wrong again. Actually, I'm no longer on active duty. I'm in the reserves."

Dana nodded.

"Didn't realize there was an Army reserve unit in Key West," he said.

"There isn't. My unit's in Miami. Criminal Investigation Department."

"Long commute. You must like it."

"One weekend a month. Sometimes more. Doesn't interfere with my regular job or anything. And, yeah, I do like it."

"Good that you keep your finger in it. What kind of work do you do? In civilian life, I mean."

"Im a cop."

"No kidding?"

"Gospel truth, a cop when I was active, a cop in the reserves and a cop here in Key West. Sounds like a broken record."

"You've obviously found your calling. Not everyone's that fortunate."

Powers considered that. Yes, she had found her calling, hadn't she?

"How about you?" she asked. "Have you found yours?"

Dana laughed.

"It found me. After Nine-Eleven, I dropped out of college to enlist. Qualified for officer's candidate school. Picked up my degree later. Lucked out getting a couple more, all courtesy of Uncle Sam."

"What are you doing now?"

"I'm with the 82nd Airborne Division in Fayetteville, North Carolina."

"So, you're here on vacation with your family?"

"Not exactly."

That was a strange answer, Powers thought. But she wouldn't pursue it. Something about this guy said he's a bigger deal than he was letting on. Better to stick with the small talk.

"I'd just graduated from college when I joined the Army," she said. "I was with the Military Police CID at Fort Belvoir, then I deployed to Iraq."

"Not a nice place. Not now and certainly not when you were there. But the Army must still have some appeal since you're in the reserves. Ever consider going active again?"

That almost startled her. How'd he know?

"It has crossed my mind," she said.

"Well, you impress me as someone we would love to have back."

The bartender brought over their coffees.

"Sorry it took so long," he apologized. "Had to make a fresh pot."

"Thank you," Powers said. "I think that'll probably be all."

"You know him?" Dana asked, nodding toward the bartender after he'd left.

"No. I've only been here a couple of times. Must've been when he was off."

"Jay Wallace. Good man. I occasionally drop by the club after work. Not much for doing the local scene. But Jay apparently knows everyone and everything going on in Key West. You should hear some of the stories he tells. Could be a source in your line of work."

Funny, Powers thought, the only *Jay* she'd ever known was Halderman.

"I'll remember that," she said. "Thank you."

"And thank you for the company," Dana said politely. "If you'll excuse me, I have to get back to my quarters. Big day tomorrow and I still have to call my wife."

"Of course," Powers smiled, surprised by his suddenness and unable to think of anything better to say.

Dana waved to the bartender and was out the door. Powers remained at the table.

"Like a refill?" Jay asked, walking over with a coffee pot. They were the only ones in the bar now.

"No, thanks. Think I'll be going, too. What do I owe you?"

"Nothing. Taken care of."

"No, no, really I can't do that. Against the rules."

"Different set of rules in here tonight. The Colonel made them."

"Who?"

"Colonel Mike Dana. Man who just left. Really nice fellow."

Well, that put the icing on this oddball evening, Powers sighed to herself. She'd been chatting up a senior officer, even flirting.

"You know him pretty well?" she asked, the cop in her coming out. "Kind of interesting his being attached to the Navy and all."

She'd guessed Dana was on assignment since he'd mentioned returning to his quarters. So he was batching it. Family must be in North Carolina. Probably lonely for him their being away.

"Just know him from his coming here," Jay said. "Rumor has it he's doing something with a SEAL team but you know how those things go."

"Yeah, scuttlebutt is scuttlebutt. Sometimes there's more to it, though. But he did mention you're pretty much up on most everything that goes on around here."

Jay laughed.

"Bartender's like a priest," he said. "Everybody talks to you."

"What about off base?" she asked. "Colonel Dana also said you were a man-about-town. Have any favorite places?"

"I'm mainly into music. Green Parrot's good. Couple of others."

Her cellphone vibrated. She slipped it out of her purse and looked at the caller. It was Jack. She let it go to message.

"Friend of mine likes the Undrinkable Bar," she said. "Not a bad music venue. Ever go there?"

"Don't believe so. I'll have to give it a try."

She took out her card and handed it to him.

"If you do, tell the bartender I'm buying you a drink."

"You're a detective," Jay said in surprise. "I thought you were an Army officer."

"That, too. Maybe we can talk again. Okay? I've got to run now."

In the parking lot, she decided to wait on returning Jack's call until she got home. There was too much on her mind at the present. She hadn't resolved a damn thing.

Chapter 21

"Car never stopped?" Billy asked. "My, my, people today."

"I don't believe the driver even realized he'd hit me," Jack said. "Although I think it might've damaged his side mirror."

"Got off lucky, Jack. Fellow was killed the other day on Duval when a truck pulled out and ran over him and his bike."

Jack had gone to the Inedible Cafe after his accident. He and Billy were sitting at a table. It looked like it was going to be a slow night.

"I should be getting my Jeep back soon," he said.

"Jeep's a toy, Jack. Truck like that one on Duval would knock you right out the other side. Need to get yourself a real car. Something big. Maybe one of those humpers."

Jack laughed and immediately grabbed at his side in pain.

"Better see about that," Billy said, concerned. "Could be hurt worser than you think."

"Little bruising's all. Just don't make me laugh. And I don't want a Hummer."

A couple of people came in.

"Bar open?" one of them asked.

"Undrinkable Bar's always open, hee, hee," Billy replied. "Make yourself comfortable and I'll be right there."

"I can take care of them," Jack offered, getting up.

"Nope," Billy said. "But why don't you join them. Have a couple of drinks and I'll call a cab to take you home. Leave that damn bicycle here. Be a lot safer for you and it."

"I'll do you one better, Billy. I'm feeling a little tired. Think I'll call the cab now. Okay to leave the bike in the kitchen?"

~~~

The stupid mirror dangled against the door. No matter how much she tried to jam it back in place, the thing would just fall out again. Not only that, it'd scratched the paint with all its flopping around. She'd have to take the car to a garage

93

and have it replaced. Perhaps she could tape it in place until she could get there.

Still, it was worth it. Though she really hadn't planned to actually hit him, just throw a little scare his way. She doubted he'd been badly injured. Serves him right, anyway. Might even teach him a lesson.

~~~

"I'm dead tired, Jack. Okay if I see you tomorrow?"

Powers had caught him the moment he'd walked through the door. He hadn't even had a chance to sit.

"Sure, I'm making it an early night myself," he said, flicking on the bathroom light. "Was at the restaurant earlier. Things are pretty slow there."

He decided not to mention the accident.

"With any luck, my car should be ready tomorrow," she said. "I know you want your Jeep back."

"No rush. It's yours as long as you need."

"I'll call you in the morning."

Jack ended the call and opened the medicine cabinet. There wasn't much inside in the way of pain killers other than a bottle of aspirin. He shook out two tablets and washed them down with a handful of cold water.

A couple of ribs on his left side had already let him know that they were unhappy and promised he'd be hearing more from them. He could prop himself up in bed with extra pillows. He knew how that would go. He'd still be in for a sleepless night, only upright.

Instead, he ran the tub full of hot water up to the top drain. Then he undressed, turned off the light and climbed in. He eased down against the back of the tub and slowly sank in up to his chin. Within minutes, he'd drifted off.

Chapter 22

Rachel Powers was up with the chickens. That's not unusual in Key West. She rolled over and looked at the bedside clock. Six a.m. The alarm was set for seven. She got out of bed anyway.

Showered, dressed and breakfasted with time to spare, she was about to leave the house when her phone rang. Caller ID was unfamiliar.

"This is Powers," she answered, as if commanding whoever it was on the other end to put up his hands.

"Detective Powers," a friendly voice replied. "This is Gary at the garage. Your car's ready to go."

~~~

"New alternator, fresh battery, two new battery cables," Gary ticked off the list. "I also replaced the fan belt. It was loose and couldn't be adjusted in tighter. Sooner or later it would've broke and there you'd be without any way to charge the battery again. Total comes to nine-hundred and fifty-five dollars. That's parts and labor."

Powers gave the car a dirty look. It appeared a little too smug for her liking.

"Wonder if you could do me a favor?" she asked, taking out her credit card.

"Sure thing."

"All right if I leave the Jeep here until my friend can come for it? I'll call him as soon as I get to work."

"No problem. Pull it around to the side over there. Nice-looking Jeep."

Powers parked the Jeep where she'd been told and hid the key under the seat. As she was leaving the lot, she noticed a car drive up with its right sideview mirror hanging off the door. She wondered how much that would cost to fix, still smarting from her repair bill.

~~~

Jack had awakened the next morning in a bathtub full of cold water. It'd taken him a moment to come to his full senses. He climbed out of the tub shivering and rubbed himself briskly with a towel to restore some circulation. His ribs complaining mightily the whole while. So much for his makeshift spa treatment, he thought. He popped a couple more aspirin.

Now feeling a little better and wrapped in a blanket, he made a pot of coffee and took it to the front room. Before settling on the sofa, he opened the door to see if the newspaper had come. It was on the porch and as he stepped out, his neighbor slowly drove past in her dark blue BMW. Something disquieting about the car flashed through his mind, causing him to take in a sharp breath. He watched it turn out of the lane and onto the main street.

There wasn't much in the paper. The usual complaints in the Citizens' Voice column – *As a taxpayer, blah, blah, blah, No one said Iguanas are the biggest issue, etc., etc.* He missed William Hackley's diary entries from 1857. It'd been dropped. Guess the old guy finally ran out of days. The thing was, he couldn't get the BMW out of his mind. He put down the paper and poured another cup of coffee.

His cellphone chimed from the bedroom. He berated himself for not bringing it out with him and braced himself to get up. To his surprise, the ribs weren't all that painful.

"Hi," Powers said. "Hope I didn't wake you."

"Been up forever. What's happening?"

"I have my car back. Left the Jeep at the garage. I can swing by after work and we can go pick it up."

"Do they have the keys?"

"Under the driver's seat."

"I'll go get it now. But swing by anyway later. We can have dinner."

"Do my best."

Again, he hadn't mentioned the accident to her. Not that he wasn't thinking about it. Just now he was wondering how much of an *accident* it'd been. He phoned for a cab.

~~~

96

Gleason was in Halderman's office when Powers walked into the detective's room. He motioned for her to join them.

"Just telling the Lieutenant about the ME's report," he said. "The lab identified that sliver Blake found in Meadows' arm. It was plastic. Smooth on two sides. Could've been from a windshield. Like maybe a motorcycle. Maybe we're looking at this thing wrong."

"Are you thinking now he was killed in a motorcycle accident?" Powers asked. "What about all those injuries? Dr. Harding was certain they were result of a fall."

"He said they were from a sudden impact," Gleason said. "Kind of thing that happens when you slam into something going fast. Especially on a bike."

"I'm not sure I buy that," Powers said, shaking her head. "There'd have been more obvious injuries. Abrasions. Broken bones. Only visible one on Meadows was at the back of his head. And it'd been enough to kill him. Others were internal."

"I'm just offering another possibility, Rachel. Truth is, a road accident is a hell of a lot more plausible than a dead man bailing out of an airplane. And it can cause a lot of internal injuries."

"We should consider what Earl is saying," Halderman put in. "Just for discussion's sake, if nothing else."

"But Lee Meadows was stark naked, sir. So, we're to think he was blowing down the highway without a stitch of clothing on? I can't believe you're serious."

"Let the man finish," Halderman admonished.

"I know it sounds improbable, Rachel," Gleason smiled. "But I've seen weirder things. Say Meadows was out of his gourd. Took off his clothes and jumped on a bike. Hit a bridge abutment straight on. Went over the side."

"He didn't own a motorcycle," Powers said quietly.

"So, he borrowed one. Stole it. You have to admit it is a possibility."

"He hit a bridge and went over the side," Powers stated. "Along with the bike, I'm assuming. Okay, then the bike should be in the water. Where do you want to start looking? How about the bridge at Garrison Bight? I suppose the body could've drifted from there around the island to Fort Zach. Let's go take a look. Got your swim trunks?"

"C'mon, Rachel," Gleason said.

"Only bridge we've got, detective, Sheriffs own the rest. By the way, anyone report a missing motorcycle?"

Halderman stood up from behind his desk.

"You kids stops arguing and get back to work," he said. "I don't want to hear any more theories. Stick with what you've got."

~~~

Jack spotted his Jeep parked in a space beside the garage. Oddly another car he thought he recognized was next to it. He paid the taxi driver and went inside to let them know he was picking up the Jeep.

"That your wheels?" the mechanic said. "Nice. Don't know if I'd have let anyone borrow it."

"She's a good driver," Jack said. "Say, that BMW out there looks like my neighbor's. Candace Farrow. I just saw her this morning. What happened?"

"Banged the side mirror on the door coming into her garage and knocked it off the mounting. Dealer would want to replace the whole mirror. I can fix it for less than half of what she'd pay for a new one. "

"Lucky she came to you," Jack said.

Back at his Jeep, he examined the damaged mirror on the BMW. It would've been at the right height, he thought. Then, it would've have been so on most cars. The more interesting thing was Candace didn't have a garage. None of the houses in the lane did.

He took a picture of the mirror with his cellphone.

Chapter 23

"**A**re you feeling all right, sir?" Powers asked Gleason They'd gone outside of the police station after Halderman had dismissed them and were standing on the sidewalk.

"Of course, I am. Why wouldn't I be?"

"That goofy motorcycle business in there. It makes no sense at all. Dr. Hardy was specific about what happened to Lee Meadow. I thought we were on the same page with this."

"I was only looking at it from another angle."

"Well, it's not a right angle," she chided. "I'd call it obtuse."

Gleason laughed. She gave him a long look.

"I have my car," she said finally. "Want to take a drive?"

"Where to?"

"Up to Marathon. We can look at bridges along the way."

"I surrender," Gleason said, holding up his hands. "My motorcycle accident theory was a stretch. Kind of like this whole damn case. But what's there to see in Marathon?"

"The airport. I also have an angle."

"Let's hear it first."

"Okay, we accept the ME's autopsy report. The victim died from a blow on the back of his head given by a specifically shaped weapon that fractured his skull. That injury was further aggravated postmortem – brains blew out the back of his head – when the body made a sudden stop after falling from a great height, say a couple thousand feet or so, which points to an airplane. The piece of plastic lodged in his arm may have come from a window in the airplane, I don't know, but not a Harley windshield."

"Stop there," Gleason said. "I agree with everything you're saying. But again, why Marathon? Why not here? Or Miami? Or East Jesus Texas?"

"All possibilities," Powers smiled. "I'd just like to start in Marathon because his truck was found there. Victor Young said he thought Meadow had moved somewhere. We know he was working in the Marathon area. Maybe he'd moved nearby to be closer."

"And you believe the airplane that dropped the body in the Florida Straits somewhere between here and Havana is at the Marathon airport, is that right?"

"Well, I have to admit East Jesus is also a strong possibility."

"Leave me in Marathon when you head for Texas. I'll catch a ride back."

~~~

"Thanks for picking me up, girlfriend."

Candace had called Amanda from the garage.

"It was good to get out of the house," Amanda said. "Drake has an all-day meeting with his partners. And frankly, I was getting bored listening to their business talk. I borrowed the Range Rover. The Lexus is in the shop."

"My car should be ready this afternoon. We can just bum around, if you want."

"I like that," Amanda said. "Hey, here's an idea. Why don't we go to Latitudes for lunch? I haven't been to Sunset Key in forever."

"You don't suppose they're full?" Candace wondered, checking her watch.

"I'm sure they can accommodate us," Amanda said, punching on the dash phone. "I'll call for reservations. It'll be a fun boat ride, too."

The usual parking lot for the restaurant was full. Amanda found another lot a few blocks away. They walked back to the pier and boarded the launch for the eight-minute trip across the harbor. It was a short walk from the dock on Sunset Key to the restaurant.

"Isn't that view something?" Amanda beamed, as they were seated. "Let's share a bottle of wine. Chardonnay good with you?"

They were on the patio overlooking the Gulf of Mexico. Only a few other tables had guests. A waiter approached and Amanda gave him their wine order.

"How're tricks?" Candace asked, after he'd left.

"You're so wicked," Amanda grinned. "Actually, I have taken on another client."

"Who is the new playmate? Anyone I'd know?"

"All I can tell you is that he calls me 'sir' and likes to be led around the room on a leash before we begin the fun and games."

"Well, you're the best, Amanda. I've always wondered, and I know this is going to sound stupid, but do you think Drake would ever get jealous?"

"I'm a professional dominatrix, for goodness sake. Drake understands that. It's business, darling."

"I know, I know. It's just when I found out about Jerry, it put me over the moon."

"Whole different animal," Amanda said.

The waiter arrived with their wine. Amanda tasted it and nodded her approval.

"Thank you," Amanda said. "We'll wait a while before we order."

Candace took a sip from her glass and looked at Amanda.

"Do you and Drake ever talk about what happened to Lee?" she asked.

"Why on earth would we? Neither of us really liked the man. He certainly wasn't anyone close."

"Guess it was his body washing up like that. Kind of upset me. I was wondering how you took it."

"The man obviously drowned," Amanda shrugged. "Frankly, I don't know how Drake felt. As far as I was concerned, it was an unfortunate accident. Not something I would've wished on him though. On anyone for that matter."

"It was just so unexpected, that's all."

"Try to forget about Lee, sugar. He wasn't a very nice person. Sure, it was shocking that he died but we move on."

"You're right, it was an unfortunate accident," Candace smiled.

Obviously, that was what her friend believed, she thought to herself. Drake was telling the truth.

"Just I've never known anyone who'd died like that," she said. "And then to have to find out in the papers. It still bugs me about the way my neighbor acted, showing up at Louie's and not saying anything when he knew all along."

"Well, Drake found out what he was up to, didn't he? That's one reason he's meeting with his partners today. I don't think we'll be hearing much from your neighbor anymore."

Candace smiled again. Maybe she was right.

~~~

Jack had driven to the Inedible Cafe to pick up his bicycle.

"Why don't you just leave that ol' thing here," Billy said. "Lot safer."

"Be just as safe at home with me," Jack said.

"Long as you stay off it, hee, hee."

Jack rolled the bike out of the kitchen to where the Jeep was parked. Billy followed.

"The car that almost run over you on Petronia," he said. "Still don't remember much about it?"

"Yeah, but I have a feeling now that it was a dark color, maybe dark blue."

"I mentioned around what'd happened to you," Billy said. "Got Sparrow to help out, too. He ran into an old fellow name of Matt Wilson who lives on Emma. Told him he was sitting on his porch when a blue car flew by like a bat out of hell. Might've been about the same time of day you were hit."

"He didn't happen to say what make of car, did he?"

"Doubt if he keeps up with these new cars. Sparrow says he's getting up in the years. Probably last thing he drove had a horse tied on the front of it, hee-hee."

So much for an eyewitness, Jack thought.

"Emma Street," he said. "That's not far from my house. Maybe I should go talk with him anyway."

"That'd be okay. He'd probably love the company. But just so you know, Sparrow also said Mister Wilson can be a little foggy sometimes, hee, hee."

Jack picked up the bicycle to put in the Jeep but a sharp pain caused him to drop it. He grabbed at his side.

"Man, that hurts," he winced. "I thought this thing was getting better."

"You better stop messing around, Jack," Billy admonished. "Go see about that shoulder before it gets worse."

"All right," Jack nodded. "Help me toss the bike in the back and I promise I'll go."

"I mean it," Billy said seriously, putting the bicycle in the Jeep himself. "That police lady friend of yours ought to know what happened, too. Might be she could do something about these maniacs driving around."

"Okay, okay, stop worrying," Jack grimaced. "I'll drive to the clinic on Truman right now."

"What about the police lady? She know?"

"I'll tell her as soon as I can."

Chapter 24

"**E**verybody runs from one end to the other?" Powers asked. "That's all?"

"Any farther and it wouldn't be the Seven Mile Bridge race," Gleason said.

They'd just crossed the bridge and were coming into Marathon.

"The downhill part shouldn't be too hard, I guess," she said, "providing you can make the uphill one."

"Piece of cake," Gleason grinned. "Airport's up ahead on the left."

"The man I spoke with said they're at the east end. Hawkes Aviation. There it is."

Powers parked and the two detectives went inside, where they were shown to the manager's office.

"Welcome to Marathon," Clayton Hawkes greeted, standing up from behind his desk. "Please have a seat."

Powers thanked him and introduced herself and Gleason.

"I understand you're looking into a possible airplane accident," Hawkes said. "I'm not sure what it is I can help you with. Generally, that would be the Feds' bailiwick."

"Actually, we're conducting a homicide investigation, sir," Powers said. "I can't give you any particulars at this point but theoretically an airplane could have been involved."

"So I'm guessing this thing took place in Key West since that's where you're from. I'd have thought you'd talk to someone at the airport there. What I'm wondering is why here?"

"It's part of a theory, sir."

~~~

Jack sat on a hard chair in the waiting area of the clinic. He'd earlier filled out the insurance and information forms at the desk and was now waiting to be called. Finally, a nurse stepped out from the hallway.

"Mr. Hunter, please come with me," she said.

Jack followed her to an examination room.

"I'm Karen Phillips, the nurse practitioner," she said, while looking at his form. "You've injured your shoulder, I see."

"Last time I was here, Doctor E-Z treated me," Jack smiled. "He still around?"

"Dr. Zisken joined Doctors Without Borders," she smiled back. "He's somewhere in Central America. Now, about your shoulder. How did you hurt it?"

"I was kind of sideswiped by a car. Caught me with his sideview mirror."

"That's terrible. Are there other injuries?"

"Just the shoulder, I think. You know, you look familiar. I'm sure I've seen you before."

Karen paused.

"It's possible," she said. "In fact, your name somehow seems familiar. Please remove your shirt."

"Yeah, it was on Margaret Street," Jack said, slowly pulling off his shirt. "I remember now. I was taking an early morning walk and passed by as you were getting out of a car."

"If you say so," she smiled. "Can you raise your arm?"

Jack put up his arm and she placed her hand on the back of his shoulder.

"There's some bruising," she said. "Try to rotate your arm. Not fast. That's good."

She next felt around his ribs.

"Ouch!" Jack complained. "Little sore around there."

"Sorry," she smiled. "Lower your arm and take a couple of deep breaths. That hurt?"

"I'm aware of it but it's not too bad," Jack answered. "What do you think?"

"I don't believe anything's broken in the shoulder area. You're lucky. A rib could be bruised or possibly cracked. I can send you to the hospital for an X-ray to make certain. There's not much you can do about the rib other than take it easy. I'll give you an elastic chest band. Take it off when you go to bed. For the shoulder, alternate cold and heat treatments. Frozen peas are great. Stick the package on top of your shoulder for about five minutes then the same with the heat pad. You can get a pad next door at the pharmacy, if you don't have one. Do these three or four times a day until you feel better. Okay?"

"Maybe a shot would help," Jack suggested.

"Only if you enjoy being stuck by a needle but you don't strike me that way. I think the frozen peas will work fine. I'll also give you a prescription for pain. "

~~~

"How could this have happened?" Amanda asked in astonishment. "It's not like we were parked in a no-parking zone. This is a private lot."

"Tow-truck driver's fault, ma'am," the parking attendant explained. "Mix-up. There was another Range Rover the same color right beside yours. Must've confused yours with it."

Amanda and Candace had returned from lunch to find their car had been mistakenly towed from the parking lot.

"But why would you have called the towing company in the first place? I told you how long we'd be. I mean, even the city wouldn't do that in the municipal lot."

"Company policy, ma'am. The other Range Rover was illegally parked. Had been here for two days. After that, we have to call the tow company. New outfit we just started using over on Stock Island. City will also tow you, by the way. 'Course they'd ticket you first. Then you'd have to pay that along with everything else."

"I guess that must mean this is my lucky day," Amanda said icily. "Didn't you go with him to make sure he got the right car? Check the license plate, all that good stuff?"

"It was time for my break. Had to leave right then. They're strict about that. Go when you're supposed to or no go. The tow-truck was gone when I got back."

Amanda put her hand to her cheek and took in a deep breath. She wanted to scream.

"This is incredible," she said. "Okay, so you went on your break. Someone must have filled in for you while you were away. Didn't you tell that person what was going on? I mean, here's somebody loading a car on a truck. He could've been stealing it for all anyone knew. Wouldn't your relief person have looked into that?"

"Oh, he knows the driver," the attendant grinned.

"My God, where do they find these people," Amanda muttered under her breath, then back to the attendant. "So where is our car now?"

"Probably at their impound lot on Stock Island. Out near Cow Key. I'll call. Tell 'em to bring it back."

"You do that, buster," she hissed. "Or else I'm calling my lawyer!"

Candace pulled her aside.

"Let's go see if my car's ready, babe," she said. "We can take a taxi to the garage and then go get yours. Fuck waiting for these jerks to get their act together."

~~~

"We can still check around the bridges for that motorcycle, sir," Powers said, passing Pigeon Key on the way back to Key West. "Thing could be in the water right under our noses."

Gleason glanced over at her.

"Actually, we did learn something," she said. "The windows in most of the planes are plastic. At least, in the little ones. That sliver in Meadow's arm might have come from an airplane door. I mean, now we're safe to assume he was dropped from a plane. Right? Everyone on board with that?"

"Yeah, but he would've had to have been kicked through the window to break the thing," Gleason argued. "Interesting about the sky-diving plane – it having a larger door would make it easier to dump him. Still doesn't explain the piece of plastic. Anyway, that airplane's engine was being rebuilt. Guy said it'd been grounded for a couple of months."

"Even with a bigger door it would be risky, though," Powers said. "The pilot would have to leave the controls to shove him out. Sounds pretty dangerous."

"Not if the pilot had help," Gleason said. "Another person on board to do the heavy lifting."

"Only way it could've happened," Powers said. "We know someone bashed in Meadow's head and that's what killed him. And we're ninety-nine percent certain that his body was dropped into the ocean from an airplane. The same someone could've committed both crimes. Knocked him off and flown the plane. But getting the body out while having to fly at the same time sounds impossible. Or near to it, anyway."

"I don't know much about airplanes," Gleason said, "but say it was a bigger plane. Not a jet but still big. Had a door in the back. Be much easier to just kick someone out of it. Could've even killed him right there in the plane."

Powers shuddered.

"So, we're looking for a murderer and an accessory," she said. "Both had to be in on it from the beginning, too. I can't imagine going out and hiring a pilot to get rid of the body after the fact."

"I wonder if they all three knew each other," she mused. "Meadow, the pilot and his little helper. Might help with motivation."

"Could be a couple," Gleason offered. "Man and woman. Meadow came between them. Love triangle gone bad."

"That's a possibility," Powers agreed. "Victor Young said Candace Farrow had kicked him out because he'd been abusive. Maybe he left because he was involved with another woman and her hubby or whatever didn't like it. Think we'll skip the bridges, if that's all right with you, sir. I'd like to get back to Key West."

~~~

The taxi dropped off the two women at the garage. Candace could see her BMW inside the work bay.

"Just finishing up," the mechanic said as they walked in. "I rubbed out the paint scratches on the door. Good as new."

"That's great," Candace said. "How much do I owe you?"

"Aw, let's make it twenty bucks," he smiled.

"I expected it to be more. Are you sure?"

"You can buy me a drink sometime."

Candace returned the smile and opened her purse.

"Met a neighbor of yours. The guy who owns that great Jeep? Noticed your Beemer and was wondering what'd happened."

The smile faded from Candace's face.

"He had no business asking," she said angrily. "What did you tell him?"

"You'd banged it against the garage, right? I didn't think it was a big deal."

"Just back my car out, please," she said.

Candace had remained silent until they were passing over the bridge to Stock Island.

"Shit!" she shouted.

Amanda jumped.

"My goodness, bunny," she laughed nervously. "You startled the life out of me. What's wrong?"

"The-guy-who-owns-the-great-Jeep," she singsonged and banged her hand on the steering wheel. "That's Jack Hunter. See? He's checking up on me again. And he knows I don't have a garage!"

"Oh, I think it was just a coincidence, hon," Amanda said. "He apparently had some work done on his car there. I don't see why that should matter. Besides, Drake has him figured out. He'll settle Mr. Hunter's hash."

"That's not the point. He was asking about *my* car."

"And?"

"And nothing. I don't like him, that's all."

Amanda gave her a curious look.

"Drake's going to have a kitten over his precious Range Rover being towed," she fretted. "They better not have damaged it."

"I think we turn here," Candace said.

Fifth Street eventually led them to an open area where the lot was located. A chain-link fence surrounded it. Ten or twelve cars were parked inside, and a small shack stood at the entrance. Two signs were fastened to the gate. One read, *ProTow*. The other, *Keep Out*. Candace parked in front and they went in.

"Can I help you?" a wiry man seated behind a desk asked.

"I want my car," Amanda told him. "It's the black Range Rover you wrongly towed from the restaurant lot in town."

The man smiled and fished out a piece of paper from a basket on the desktop.

"Oh, yeah, just brought it in," he said. "The charge is one hundred and eighty dollars."

"I beg your pardon," Amanda said. "There should be no charge. You took the wrong car. Didn't they tell you?"

"Nobody told me anything, ma'am."

"But they called you. You were supposed to return the car."

"The only call I got was to come and tow a Range Rover. The paperwork's right here in the computer. Range Rover. Color black. License number RPLAYR. That's kind of cute. What's it mean?"

"It means mind your own business," Amanda snapped. "Now, may I have the keys and we can be on our way?"

"Soon's you pay your bill."

"You've got to be kidding," Amanda said, coughing a little laugh. "That's outrageous!"

"No, ma'am, it's the going rate. That includes a hundred thirty-five for the tow, forty five bucks an hour for the driver's time and taxes. Cash, if you please. Can't take plastic. Machine's broke."

"Well, I'm not paying you a fucking cent," Amanda said, eyes flashing angrily. "Cash or plastic. You towed the wrong car, buster, so it's your problem."

"Not my problem at all, ma'am," the man shrugged. "We contract with the parking lot. Any dispute you can take up with them. But right now, you owe me one hundred and eighty dollars. It'll be twenty-five more tomorrow for storage. And another twenty-five the day after that. And so on down the line. Like they say, time is money."

"How much do you have, babe?" Candace asked, reaching into her purse while glaring at the man.

"Don't be silly, sweetheart," Amanda scoffed. "I'm not giving this crook a dime!"

"Just pay the stupid thing and let's get the hell out of here," Candace said tightly. "I've got eighty-five...wait, here's another ten."

Amanda threw up her hands in disgust.

"Fuck!" she said, snapping open her purse. "We need eighty-five more. Here it is. Give me yours."

She counted out the money and placed the stack of bills on the desk. A twenty skidded off and onto the floor.

111

Robert Coburn

"You can pick that up yourself," she said.

Chapter 25

Jack pulled his best imitation of a baboon face – eyes wide, teeth bared. His Jeep had fallen in behind a Conch Train and the two kids riding in the back car had immediately made a face at him. To their delight he'd made one back and the game was on. Their parents had gotten in on the fun by taking photos of the three of them over the past four blocks.

Sadly for everyone, the train turned left at Windsor Lane. Jack tooted his horn and waved at the children as he passed. He continued up Truman and turned left himself, on Pohalski, which became Ashe a block later and where Ruth LaVere and Bobby Sunshine lived. He'd been meaning to look in on Ruth since she'd been ill earlier.

He parked at the curb and sat for a moment. The little house held scores of memories, many sweet and dear. It had taken him in during a rough time. Friends – some having moved on, others still around – had entered his life there. Then there were memories not so pleasant. Such as the night he'd been ambushed and shot by a drug dealer on its front porch. Ruth was puttering in the flower bed.

"Sorry, the room's been rented," she crabbed good-naturedly, as he walked up.

Jack offered his hand to help her get to her feet. The effort earned a chorus of complaints from his ribs.

"Throw the bum out," he said. "I hear he writes bad checks. Looks like you're feeling better. That so?"

"It was just allergies."

"Bobby said it was a nasty cold and had gone to your chest. He was worried."

"Oh, hush," she scoffed. "Pay no attention to his nonsense."

"Well, I don't blame him. A thing like that could turn into pneumonia."

"Let's go inside. Roy will want to see you."

Jack followed her in.

113

"You have a visitor, Roy," Ruth announced.

The African Grey Parrot ruffled its feathers and rocked back and forth on its perch.

"Got a song for me?" Jack cooed.

The bird rocked some more but remained silent.

"His beak's out of joint," Ruth said. "Bobby scolded him."

"Why? What did he do?"

"Happened when I had this terrible cough. Roy liked the sound and picked up on it. You know how he can be. Anyway, with the two of us hacking every other minute, it eventually got on Bobby's nerves."

Jack couldn't help but laugh.

"Bobby mentioned something about that," he said. "But it's so unfair. He's a parrot. That's what they do."

"Roy will get over it. Just looking for attention."

"C'mon, Roy," Jack said, leaning closer to the cage. "Let's do a duet."

Jack sang softly the opening lyrics from *My Funny Valentine*. Roy turned his back to him.

"Well, I guess that's *that*," Jack smiled, straightening up. "Where is Bobby, by the way?"

"He's checking on his boat. Thinking about selling it."

"Selling it? He loves the boat. What's going on?"

Ruth shook her head.

"His dad needs a knee replacement," she said. "Been hobbling on it for years. Finally decided to have it looked at. New insurance policy he bought claims it's a pre-existing condition. Say they won't cover it."

"Doesn't he have Medicare?"

"Never signed up. Considers it socialism."

"That is so much bullshit," Jack said. "Ask Bobby to call me before he does anything drastic. Look, I better be going home."

Jack gave Ruth a hug and left. A tiny voice trailed after him from inside the house...*bullshit*.

~~~

"But you haven't pinned down exactly where the airplane came from, is that right?"

Gleason and Powers were in Halderman's office after having driven back from Marathon.

"We aren't even sure what kind of airplane it was, Lieutenant," Gleason said. "The guy at the airport showed us one that skydivers use. Had a big door for them to jump out of so it'd be easy to drop a body as well."

"Yes, but the pilot would have to crawl back there," Powers added. "Could get dicey with no one being at the controls. However, Detective Gleason suggested he might've had help. So, we're looking at a possible second party. Also, it could've been a larger plane than the skydivers. Like a passenger airplane. As far as where it came from, it could be anywhere from Key West to Miami. Maybe beyond, although I still favor Marathon since that's where Meadow's truck was found."

"What about the vic's friends?" Halderman asked. "Any more on them or should I say any more of them?

"From what we know about the guy, he wasn't much of a social figure in Key West," Gleason said. "More of a loner. We still haven't gotten up with the ex-girlfriend, Candace Farrow. Keep missing her at her home. Either she's avoiding us or bad timing on our part."

"Hmm, and Jack Hunter hasn't seen anything of her, Rachel?" Halderman asked. "He lives right down from her house, right?"

Gleason smiled to himself.

"I haven't spoken with him today," she answered coolly, glancing at Gleason. "Next time I see him, though, I'll ask."

"Okay," Halderman said. "Do another run on the bars in town. See if he had any drinking buddies. He definitely impressed someone enough to kill him."

~~~

Jack removed the packet of frozen peas from his shoulder. It felt better. The ribs were no longer complaining unless he made a sudden move. He should've had the prescription filled. He carefully stood up and went to the kitchen to put the peas back in the freezer.

On the way home after visiting Ruth, he had driven down to Candace's house. There'd been no car parked in the drive.

It'd also appeared that no one was at home. The side of the house hadn't shown any sign of the car having bumped into it either, if that was what the mechanic had meant.

He took out his cellphone and scrolled to the picture he'd taken of the damaged mirror. Then he grabbed up the Jeep keys. And just as quickly changed his mind. He would walk instead. Emma Street wasn't that far away.

Jack had no problem finding the address Billy had given him. And as luck would have it, an older gentleman was sitting on the front porch of the tiny house. His hair topped his head in a snow-white fuzzy ball. It made Jack wonder if it might blow off like a dandelion.

"Good afternoon, sir," he called to the man. "Are you Mister Matt Wilson?"

"Can't say" the man answered with a chuckle. "Depends on who wants to know?"

"My name's Jack Hunter," Jack answered. "I'm a friend of Billy Bean and Sparrow Lovewell."

"You the fellow got hit by the car? Sparrow said you were knocked off your bicycle. Lucky you weren't hurt worse."

"Yes, sir, that's what happened," Jack said. "And you're right. I was lucky. Wonder if you could spare me a moment to talk about that car."

"Come on up and have a seat."

Jack climbed the steps and pulled the chair closer to the old gent.

"I remember it well," Wilson said. "Came flying down the street going much too fast for the neighborhood. People living here have children and pets. But then, folks are always driving in a big hurry these days, aren't they? So, you think it might've been the one that hit you and drove off?"

"It's possible," Jack said. "I believe it was a dark blue color. Does that ring a bell?"

"The car I saw was dark. Could've been blue. Hard to say for sure."

"Any idea of the driver? Man or woman?"

"I really couldn't tell."

"Don't suppose you know the make, huh?"

Billy's comment about the man's age came to Jack's mind. Said he was getting foggy, too. Could have dementia. He didn't expect to learn much. Although, the old guy seemed pretty sharp so far.

"It was a BMW," Wilson said.

"Are you sure?" Jack asked, completely surprised.

"I know car makes pretty well. Worked for a while at General Motors in the 'fifties. Was a chauffeur before I retired. Always liked BMW's. Same initials as mine, you see – B...M...W."

He paused and gave Jack a grin.

"Stands for Bartholomew Matthew Wilson. That's my full name. My folks named me after the Apostles. They couldn't do much about our family name. No 'w's'."

"That's absolutely amazing," Jack said.

"Kind of funny. I always think about that when I see one of those cars."

Jack took out his cellphone and showed him the car's picture.

"I've a feeling that this might be the one you saw speeding. What do you think?"

"That looks like the color all right," Wilson said, then taking a closer look. "Don't know about the mirror hanging down. Can't remember seeing that."

"It would've been on the opposite side passing you. Broke off when it clipped me."

Wilson studied the photograph a moment longer.

"You know, the more I think about it now," he said, "I believe it could've been a lady driving that car."

~~~

"I don't know if I'm up for barhopping on Duval tonight," Gleason said. "It's been a busy day. Let's put it on our dance card for tomorrow. That'll keep the lieutenant happy."

"No argument from me, sir," Powers said.

The two detectives were standing in the police station parking lot. A couple of officers arriving for the next shift waved as they passed.

"Personally, I doubt if we'll find anything on Duval," she added, "but here's a thought. What about looking in on the outskirts. You know, neighborhood bars, shopping centers, that sort of thing."

"Lot of driving but it's not a bad idea. We can map it out first thing in the morning. Meanwhile, I'm going home and then out for a run."

"How's that coming, sir?"

"Knocked another couple of minutes off my time."

"Awesome."

Gleason got in his car and Powers walked over to where she'd parked. Her cellphone chimed. She recognized the number.

"Hi, just leaving work. What's up?"

"Bad, good and interesting news," Jack said. "Too much to talk about over the phone. Be better over dinner."

"Hmm, sounds mysterious. I have to change clothes first."

"Stella by Starlight okay? I can pick you up or meet you there."

"I'll meet you there. If you come here, we'll never get away."

"Now you're talking."

"Meet you there in an hour."

She ended the call and smiled. Three kinds of news, she thought. Well, bad news came second nature to Jack. Part of his charm, she'd joked. And good news was up to interpretation when it involved him. *Interesting*, however, was an unfamiliar category. Made her wonder.

She checked her watch. She'd have to hurry.

~~~

Jack felt excited about what he'd learned from Matt Wilson. He rubbed his cheek. He'd better shave. He would grab a quick shower, too.

Five minutes later he was toweling off and deciding what to wear. He opted for a light sweater over a tee-shirt and jeans. The evenings had been cool over the past few days.

Dressed to the nines by Key West standards, he stepped off the front porch and threw a quick glance down the lane before continuing. A blue BMW was parked in the drive next to Candace's house. He turned around and went back inside.

~~~

Detective Rachel Powers pulled up behind the BMW, effectively blocking it. She'd barely gotten home when Jack's call came. On the breakneck drive back across town, she'd phoned Gleason but had gotten only his voice mail. She decided not to leave a message. She'd fill him in afterwards.

She was about to knock on the door for the third time when a woman's face appeared in the window.

"Who is it?" she called from behind the glass.

"Police, ma'am," Powers said and held up her ID.

The face disappeared and a few seconds later the door opened partially.

"Is there something wrong?" the woman asked.

"Good afternoon," Powers smiled. "I'm Detective Rachel Powers with the Key West Police Department. Are you Candace Farrow?"

Candace hesitated.

"Uh ... yes, what's this about?"

"It concerns Lee Meadow," Powers said. "I understand he lived here. May I come in?"

Candace paused again.

"I was just leaving," she said. "Could we do this another time?"

"I think it would be better if we talked now, ma'am."

"All right," Candace said reluctantly, opening the door completely.

"Thank you," Powers said, stepping in. "This won't take long, I promise."

Candace motioned her to a chair while she took a seat on the sofa.

"My, what a cute place," Powers said, looking around the room. "Are you a decorator?"

"I give decorating advice," Candace said.

"Boy, could I use some of that," Powers laughed. "My house is furnished in early Goodwill."

Candace studied Powers.

"You look familiar," she said with a frown.

"Really? I don't believe we've met before. And I'm pretty good on faces."

Candace shrugged.

"Whatever. So you wanted to ask about Lee?"

"First, I want to express my condolences. Had you two been together long?"

"Not very. We weren't close."

"Really? But he did live here with you."

"It was only until he found somewhere else."

Powers raised her eyebrows in surprise.

"Are you saying he was just a roomer? There was no romantic interest involved?"

Candace shrugged again.

"How did you meet?"

"In a bar. Where else in Key West?"

"And he told you he was looking for a room to rent? I've heard some great pickup lines, but I have to say that tops the list. Am I missing a step here?"

Candace appeared agitated. She shifted around in the chair.

"I'm not trying to pry into your personal business, Miss Farrow," Powers said. "I'm just looking to get a fix on Lee Meadow. So far, we haven't had much luck. Be great if you could help me out."

"Okay, so we started seeing each other." Candace admitted. "Eventually, he wanted it to be more, so I let him move in."

"Why didn't you just say that?" Powers asked. "People live together all the time. Nothing wrong with it."

"I just felt funny about telling you," Candace said sheepishly. "Guess I'm old fashioned. I must've gotten that from my mom."

Powers smiled. Her impression of this woman was anything but old-fashioned.

"So, why did you break up?" she asked.

"It just turned out we really didn't have all that much in common. We agreed it'd be better if we went our separate ways."

"Was there ever any violence between you and him?" she asked in a confidential tone. "I know sometimes that's embarrassing to talk about but did he ever hit you?"

"No, I wouldn't have put up with that."

"He was okay with simply calling it quits?"

"Not much he could do about it even if he wasn't," Candace said breezily. "It's my house, after all."

Powers nodded.

"Well, that's one way of putting it," she said. "Guess there was no reason for him to come back for anything, right?"

Candace shook her head.

"Nope. He completely cleared out."

"Do you know where he moved? This is the last address we have on him."

"We didn't keep in touch. And like you said, there was no reason for him to come back."

"I don't suppose you know if he had any family," Powers said. "We haven't been able to locate anyone."

"He never mentioned his family to me. He wasn't all that outgoing. Besides, it's not like we were best friends."

"Did he have any interests or hobbies?" Powers asked.

"He collected junk nobody wanted and left it all over the place."

"Did you have mutual friends you saw? In either of your circles?"

"He never mentioned his friends. As far as my friends went, he was indifferent, and the feeling was mutual."

"How about enemies, then?" Powers asked. "Do you know of any reason someone would've wanted to harm him? Did he do drugs, for example, and owe money?"

"You mean owe a drug dealer?" Candace said. "None of us did drugs. I don't know why anyone would've wanted to hurt him. Lee drowned. It was an accident. Why are the police are so involved?"

"Our job is to make certain it was an accident," Powers said. "We're treating it as a suspicious death for the present time. Until evidence proves differently that will continue to be the course of our investigation."

Candace looked stunned. She opened her mouth to say something but could only manage to clear her throat.

"You've been very helpful," Powers said, standing and handing her a card. "And if you do think of anything else, please call."

Candace replied with a crumpled smile.

She watched Powers get into her car and pull away. Then she saw the car stop in front of Jack Hunter's house. Jack came out to the car and they spoke for a moment, then she drove off again.

And then Candace remembered where she'd seen Rachel Powers before.

Chapter 26

This time Gleason answered his phone.

"Powers, sir. I just finished interviewing Candace Farrow. Kind of interesting. I'm not far from you. Can we get together?"

She'd cancelled her dinner plans with Jack and was about to turn onto Olivia Street.

"How do you feel about nuked pizza?" Gleason said.

"My all-time favorite."

"Come on up."

~~~

Jack had decided to walk to the Inedible Cafe. Certainly, he'd been disappointed about missing out on the evening but had understood the urgency of her having to meet with Gleason.

He did wonder what she'd found out from Candace that was so important, however. He'd had his own opinion of the woman before the accident. Now he was more than ever convinced she'd been the one who had hit him. The question remaining in his mind was why?

A few people were in the restaurant as Jack entered. A couple more at the Undrinkable Bar.

"Jack," Billy said. "Good thing you're here. Want you to meet our new bartender."

Billy led him back to the bar.

"Albena, this is Jack Hunter," he said.

She was an extremely attractive woman, tall and with long brunette hair that fell below her shoulder.

"Glad to meet you," Jack said. "The Al stand for Alice?"

"Albena is my first name," she smiled.

"Ask her to mix you a martini, Jack. Does it perfect right down to the last drop, hee-hee."

"I'm not much of a martini man, Albena. They go straight to my head."

"Then I'll mix you a chocolate one. It takes a little longer to get there."

~~~

Mitts had settled comfortably on Powers' lap. Purrs rumbled from him.

"I thought he'd be skittish with a stranger," Gleason remarked.

"He's just a good judge of character," Powers smiled, stroking the cat's head.

The three of them were out on the deck. Night noises had begun to pick up. A siren wailed from somewhere distant. Another echoed.

"How many sets of tires do you suppose the fire department runs through a year?" Gleason asked.

"About as many as we do," Powers said.

"Sorry to have missed your call," Gleason said. "Out taking a run. Had the phone on vibrate. Didn't feel a thing."

"Probably better there was just one of us there, sir. She might've thought we were ganging up on her."

"Still, I'd like to have talked with her," Gleason said. "So, you think she's hiding something?"

Mitt hopped down to inspect something at the edge of the deck.

"She was evasive to say the least," Powers said. "Also, her story didn't quite match up with her neighbor's. Victor Young said that he'd seen Lee Meadow slap her around, yet she never mentioned any violence, even when I asked her straight out."

"Women often don't," Gleason said. "It's how the society is."

"I know that, sir. But this was *me* doing the asking. Usually, women are more willing to talk with another woman. Also, I pointed out that I could understand her embarrassment, if that was holding her back."

"You want another slice of pizza?" Gleason asked. "Plenty left."

"No, thanks, I'm good. Couple of other things about her. At first, she insisted that Meadow was nothing more than a lodger. He was merely renting a room until he found somewhere else. That didn't make any sense to me. Why move there if you weren't planning to stay. She insisted that no hanky-panky was involved."

Mitts meowed and thundered back across the deck to inside the apartment, startling Powers.

"Don't worry," Gleason laughed. "Just part of his act."

"Does he do that often?"

"Now and then. Something about that tree. I believe we were talking about hanky-panky?"

"Yes, I pressed her on that and she finally admitted that there had been a relationship between them but that she'd broken it off. Said they had nothing in common."

"They had to live together to find that out?" Gleason asked. "I suppose it's possible."

"I thought it a little strange, too," Powers said. "I asked how had they met and she told me it was in a bar."

"Didn't say which bar?"

"No, but since Meadow had been so anxious to move in, you'd think he wouldn't been too happy about being kicked out. When I asked how he'd taken it, she shrugged it off. Said it was her house. Like it or lump it."

"Pretty cold to me," Gleason said.

"And that's exactly how she came across to me," Powers agreed. "I mean right from the beginning she started putting him down. Oh, and she said that he'd cleared out all of his stuff when he left. Wasn't coming back. Ever. No need to stay in touch. Yet, he had a key to the house. And here's another thing. I asked about his family, friends or any mutual ones. She claimed he didn't have any. So then I asked if he were into drugs. Owed a dealer and couldn't pay. Ridiculous, she scoffed. Said they didn't use drugs. However, I got the impression she wasn't referring to Lee when she said *they* but to others."

"Interesting."

"I think so, too. She made a big deal wanting to know why I was even asking because as far as she knew he'd drowned. Obviously an accident. That was when I told her that we were looking at the cause of death as suspicious."

Gleason gave a little grunt.

"How'd she react to that?" he asked.

"Speechless. I think it really shook her up."

Both detectives sat quietly for a moment. Mitts returned to the deck.

"Personally, I believe she was straight out lying about almost everything," Powers said.

"That was good work, Rachel. Candace Farrow is all we have right now. We'll focus on her. Try to find some of those elusive friends."

"Maybe Jack could help somehow since he's her neighbor," Rachel offered. "He could at least keep an eye on her."

"It's getting a little cool," Gleason said, ignoring the suggestion. "You want to go inside?"

"Actually, I have to be leaving, sir. Thanks for dinner."

~~~

Drake Boynton sat by his pool staring into the dark water.

He'd earlier discovered the airplane's windscreen was missing from the back of the Range Rover. How long it'd been gone he could only guess but he was certain it'd been there the last time he'd used the car.

It was all Amanda's fault, of course. If only she hadn't borrowed the Range Rover. And then the incredibly bad luck that'd followed. Jesus Christ!

Something splashed in the pool. He should've turned on the lights. But then Amanda would've wanted to join him and at the moment, he preferred to be alone. He needed to think.

He refilled his wine glass.

Either someone at the parking lot or the impound yard took the damn thing. That had to be it. He doubted the idiots at the parking lot would be stealing from the cars there. Too many people around. His money was on the impound yard. The jerk sounded shady enough, considering what he'd charged Amanda. Also, he's out in the middle of nowhere. He ought to drive there and confront the thieving bastard, call the police.

And what then? He had no proof. The guy would probably just shrug him off. Also, making a big stink might raise questions. Let things stay the way they were.

He went inside for another bottle of wine. He'd turn on the pool lights while he's there, too. Time to make peace with Amanda.

Chapter 27

"**D**etective Gleason, this is Sheriff's Deputy Don Perry up in Marathon. Surprised you're in so early. Must get up with those Key West chickens down there."

Gleason laughed.

"What can I do for you, Deputy Perry?"

Gleason had indeed come in to work earlier than usual. The conversation with Powers the evening before had kept him awake for most of the night. He'd been reading through the murder book for Lee Meadow when the deputy rang.

"Actually, detective, I have something on that truck the kids took joyriding," Perry said.

Gleason slid his notepad closer and picked up a pen.

"I remember you now, Deputy Perry," Gleason said. "And thanks again for letting us have the truck. We're treating the case as a homicide now."

"Then maybe this will help in your investigation," Perry said. "Got a burglary call from a local business near Boot Key Harbor. Place sells marine electronic equipment. Radios, fish finders, radar, you name it. Pricey stuff. Anyway, the owner recently installed a high-end surveillance system. He believed he was getting some unauthorized visitors and decided to step up his game. This time he got some nice video of the thief breaking in the back door. Odd thing was he first tried using a key. When that didn't work, he forced it. Then once inside, another camera saw him picking up some very expensive electronics. Even glanced up at the lens a couple of times. I tell you, they don't make crooks as smart as they used to anymore."

"Sounds like you've got your man," Gleason said.

"We sure do," Perry laughed. "He used to work there. Explains his having the key. Didn't realize the locks had been changed. We have a warrant for his arrest and have put out a be-on-the-lookout. You've probably got the BOLO by now."

"Our patrol would be on it," Gleason said. "So, where does this fit in with our case?"

"Just about to get to that," Perry said. "The outside camera on the back of the building covers a small parking area and also includes some of the street. While I was looking at the pictures, it occurred to me that this was the same street where those kids found the truck. I asked the shop owner how far back did the recordings go."

Powers came into the detective's room, sat down at her side of the desk.

"Don't tell me you've got the truck on the tape," Gleason said.

"Exactly that and more," Perry said. "And it's not tape, by the way. This new stuff is all digital. You can record a ton of surveillance with much better picture quality."

"Amazing times we live in, deputy," Gleason chuckled. "You mentioned something about having more?"

"I've a feeling we might have a picture of the truck when it was dropped off."

Gleason reached across the desk and gave Powers a fist bump.

"We'll be there in an hour, Deputy Perry," he said.

"What was that all about?" Powers asked, as he hung up the phone.

"I'll explain it on the way. Let's go."

~~~

Jack had discovered that too much chocolate can indeed be a bad thing. But he did have to hand it to Albena. She knew how to mix a martini. Or two. Or even three.

It was the second one that'd snuck up and sweet-talked him into having just one more. And three was the charm. He'd hung around for a little while talking with Billy before leaving. He'd considered calling Rachel once he'd gotten home, on the off chance they could still have dinner but had come to his senses before doing anything stupid and went straight to bed.

Now he was up and about, thanks to the resident rooster, and having a cup of coffee on the small front porch. It was a fine Key West morning. He took out his phone and punched in Power's number.

"Yes?" she answered.

"Wondering if we could have that dinner tonight," he said. "Like to run something past you concerning my neighbor."

Powers really didn't want to talk to Jack with Gleason in the car, but she was too curious to let that pass.

"Can you tell me now? Short version?"

"Sounds crazy but I think it's possible she might've tried to kill me."

Powers hesitated before replying.

"What happened?" she asked.

"I was knocked off my bike by a car. Didn't stop. Not sure but I think it was her."

"When was this? Did you report it?"

"Couple of days ago and no, I didn't. It was a hit and run. I was okay."

"Where are you now?"

"At home."

"Stay there. I'm in Marathon. I'll call as soon as we get back. Bye."

They were crossing the Seven Mile Bridge. Gleason looked over to her as she pocketed her cellphone.

"That our mutual friend?" he asked.

"Yes, he'd had an accident. He's all right."

"Accident's his middle name," Gleason said.

Powers gave him a look.

"Sheriffs station's up ahead," she told him. "Try not to drive past."

Gleason smiled and a minute later had pulled into the lot. The two detectives went inside the station and were met by Sheriff's Deputy Don Perry.

"Right on time," he said, looking at his wristwatch. "Always appreciated punctuality."

"They say timing's everything," Gleason laughed. "This is my partner, Detective Rachel Powers."

"Glad to meet you, sir," Powers said, offering her hand.

"A pleasure, ma'am," he said with a courtly nod.

Perry led them to a small room where a laptop computer rested on a table.

"I downloaded the security camera's information for the past two months," he said, booting up his computer. "Here's the part I think you'll like. About five weeks in."

An image of the dimly lit parking lot and street flashed on the screen. Headlights illuminated the scene as a truck drove into the top of the frame and parked at the curb a few feet in front of the lot's entrance. The time and date was superimposed at the bottom of the screen.

"That's Meadow's truck!" Powers exclaimed excitedly. "Look, you can see the license plate. WHIPIT."

Another vehicle stopped in the street next to the truck but was partially blocked from view.

"Who the hell's that?" Gleason said.

The truck's interior light came on as someone exited and then went out. A moment later the unidentified vehicle drove off.

"Wow!" Powers said and exchanged a glance with Gleason.

"You said this is two months' worth of tape? Gleason asked. "I mean digital whatever."

"That's right, detective," Perry said. "The camera's only on at night. Other thing is they hooked it up to a motion detector, so it only turns on when it thinks it sees something. We can run through the earlier dates, if you want. A couple of different vehicles have parked in that space, but this is the first time the truck showed up. From then on it remained there. That is until those kids decided to take it joyriding."

"How're they making out?" Gleason chuckled.

"Oh, they're good kids," Perry said. "Got them in the Sheriffs Explorer program."

"I'd like a copy of this video, if you could," Gleason said, pointing at the computer.

"No problem, detective. I'll shoot it down to you. This is probably my last case. After thirty-five years of driving the beat, my wife and I are going to take a long vacation."

"So you're pulling the pin?" Gleason smiled.

"Yes, sir. Thinking of renting an RV and seeing some of the country."

"Have any plans for after that?" Gleason asked.

"My wife's younger brother owns a security company up in Homestead. Handles a couple of shopping malls, few other places. Also does private work for individual protection. Probably go to work for him."

Gleason nodded.

"Well, the best of luck to you, Deputy Perry," he said. "And thanks for your help here. We really do appreciate it."

"I have one question, sir, before we go," Powers said. "You mentioned that you had downloaded the camera's information. Do you know how it was originally stored? That is, say, on a card?"

"I'd say a card since it's a new system," Perry said. "You can store a mountain of info on one and not lose integrity. The camera sends what it has to the store's computer and they probably keep everything in a Cloud account."

"Well, that's what I was thinking, too," Powers said. "I'd like to see if there's any way of isolating the area where the truck is parked. Crop out the rest of the lot and maybe enhancing the picture. We might be able to pick up something from that second vehicle."

Perry scratched his head.

"I'm sure the store's owner would cooperate," he said. "I'll call our crime lab and see what they think. One thing for certain, they have a much better monitor than mine."

"Maybe we'll finally get lucky," Powers said.

~~~

Staying home, as he'd been asked to do, had a short life. After an hour of it, Jack had decided to drive over to Ruth's house and look in on Bobby Sunshine. However, once there, he'd found out that Bobby had gone to Stock Island. Something about his boat, Ruth had said.

He parked the Jeep near the slip where the *Joyful Noise* was berthed. Bobby was sunning in a chair on the aft deck. He looked asleep.

"Ahoy!" Jack yelled. "Permission to come aboard?"

"Who's there?" Bobby said, obviously startled awake.

"Me," Jack said, stepping down onto the deck. "Sorry to disturb your dreams."

"Just catching a wink," Bobby said, stretching and getting to his feet. "Been busy all morning cleaning. Got a fellow coming by this afternoon wants to see it."

"Heard you were putting her on the market."

"Yep," Bobby said, folding his arms. "Getting too old to be galivanting around the high seas anymore."

Jack laughed.

"You never were a good liar," he said. "Ruth told me your dad needed an operation. That what this is all about?"

"Ruth's just making more out of something than it is," Bobby huffed. "I'd already decided to sell the boat. Hardly ever take her out. Just setting here eating up money."

Jack walked over to the side and looked down at the water.

"What are you asking?"

"Hoping to get twenty thousand."

Jack whistled.

"Okay, if I go inside?" he asked. "Like to look around one more time."

"Sure, Jack. I'll get us a beer."

It was just as Jack had remembered, of course – the salon paneled in polished cherry wood, as if done by a professional cabinetmaker. Sleeping quarters in the forward section.

Bobby grabbed a couple of beers from the refrigerator. Gave one to Jack and popped open his own.

"Here's to better times, Jack."

"What's the rent on the slip?" Jack asked.

"Little less than a house in Old Town," Bobby chuckled, adding. "Pleasure boats for the money crowd today. Might be different if she was still a working boat and I was out crabbing."

Jack noticed a bitter tone. It wasn't like Bobby.

"Couldn't you do that again? he asked. "Believe you said you'd changed the rear deck. Shouldn't be too hard to put it back the way it was, would it?'

"Been away from crab fishing too long, Jack. Can't change that. Better to just move on."

Jack took in the wonderful wood paneling again.

"Well, if you're bound and determined to sell, Bobby, I think the Joyful Noise is worth a lot more than twenty grand. I'd say twice that."

Bobby suddenly looked as if the weight of years had fallen upon him. Jack was saddened and felt a certain pity for his old friend.

"Maybe so, Jack, maybe so. But I want a quick deal."

"That doesn't mean you have to give it away. Why the rush?"

"Personal reason, Jack. Rather not get into it."

The two men stood quietly for a moment. A clamor of gulls rose from outside and then just as quickly faded.

"Tell you what, Bobby," Jack said at last. "You want a quick deal? How about I give you a good deal instead."

Bobby shook his head.

"I'm not looking for charity, Jack, if that's what you're getting at. You're a real friend. In fact, Ruth and I think of you as more than that."

Jack held up his palms in protest.

"This is strictly business, Bobby, charity has nothing to do with it. I'll buy your boat for forty thousand dollars. But with a proviso. You're still the captain. Same as if it's your boat. What do you say?"

Bobby looked away for a moment, then turned back.

"I don't know what to say, Jack."

"You've never been lost for words since I've known you, Bobby. Just say it's a deal."

"It's a deal," Bobby said with a catch in his voice.

Jack stuck out his hand and they shook on it. Bobby immediately brightened. He was back to being his old self. Jack felt relieved.

"Kind of exciting being a boat owner," Jack smiled. "Anything I should know, Bobby?"

"It'd probably be a good idea to have her hauled out for a bottom re-fitting. Wouldn't wait too long. Been a while since the last one. There's a good yard in Garrison Bight. I can run her over for you, Jack. Pricey but you get what you pay for."

Bobby was indeed his old self again.

Chapter 28

Gleason hadn't spoken two words since leaving Marathon. Powers had chattered on and on about the possibility of finding something new on the security camera but all he'd done was grunt in reply. Now they were passing through Boca Chica. She couldn't stand it any longer.

"I hope Mitts will give you back your tongue, sir."

"What?"

"You've been awfully quiet. Something wrong?"

Gleason gave an embarrassed laugh.

"Sorry. I was thinking about Perry."

"Who?"

"Don Perry," Gleason said irritated. "The Sheriff's Deputy we just saw."

Powers was surprised at his reaction.

"All right. Don Perry. What about him?"

"Nothing," Gleason said. "Just what he said about retiring. You ever think what you'll do after you get out of this damn business?"

"I really can't say that I have, sir. I mean, it's not like it's happening anytime soon."

"Yeah, I guess you're right. Didn't mean to sound off."

"But I suppose it is something to think about," Powers smiled. "Have to face it eventually."

"The Lieutenant says he's planning to put in his papers next year," Gleason said. "Don't know how serious he is, though."

"How long has he been with the department?"

"He'll have twenty-five years then. See, that's just it. He could go another five with no problem. Do thirty, maybe make captain and get a better package."

"Or maybe he just doesn't want to," Powers said. "He could have another job waiting, too."

"Yeah, like Perry," Gleason sneered. "Doing the shopping mall shuffle. I just can't see myself doing that, can you?"

"Actually, Perry might be on to something," Powers said. "That security company sounds like it's a pretty big operation. Anyway, retirement's too far ahead for me to worry about. Did the Lieutenant say who'll take over?"

Gleason hesitated before answering. Should he tell her the LT had him in mind, he wondered? He decided to play it safe for now and leave it open.

"Probably be up to the brass," he said.

"Well, the only person I can think of who's qualified in detectives would be you, sir."

"Nice of you to say but I'm not so sure. Truth is, the LT is pushing me to take the exam."

"You really should think about that, sir. It'd be a great move for you."

Gleason laughed.

"Then I'd have to team you up with Sonny Breaks," he said.

Powers groaned.

"And then you'd be looking for another detective, sir."

Although, she thought, he might have to start looking before then.

~~~

Amanda Boynton had a noon appointment scheduled with a new client. She was still upset over the unpleasant incident at the towing company. She was happy the Lexus was back. She would use it today. Drake was fine with that. He had a meeting himself in Shark Key later in the day concerning some investments and would take the Range Rover. He preferred it anyway, he'd always joked, because the car was so much like himself, rugged yet refined. He'd say that with a naughty wink.

However, he hadn't mentioned the business in Shark Key was second on his list. First, there was a matter in Cow Key to see about.

He'd changed his mind after last night. He should've realized that he couldn't just do nothing. It was a loose end and it needed tying up.

The man running the tow company was obviously dishonest, however, that didn't mean he was unreasonable.

He would simply appeal to that side of his nature. Offer him money. No questions asked. No need for threats.

He angled off the highway at MacDonald Avenue and turned onto Fifth Street. A tow truck passed him heading in the opposite direction. He hoped the driver wasn't the guy he wanted to see. He continued down Fifth and parked on the roadside by the lot's office building.

~~~

Gleason and Powers had gone straight into Halderman's office to update him on their findings in Marathon.

"You ought to buy a lottery ticket today," Halderman said, shaking his head. "The guy's truck being caught on the tape. How lucky is that?"

"We take what we can get," Gleason grinned.

"It's not tape, Lieutenant," Powers put in. "It's digital. Better picture. We're hoping the Sheriffs crime lab can pull up more detail and maybe even more information outside the normal framing. We might even see the car that picked up the driver."

"Be lucky to get it back anytime soon without having a rush order for the lab," Gleason said.

"Yeah, more like just get in line with everyone else," Halderman. "Anyone have any clout with them?"

"I've used up all of mine," Gleason laughed. "Maybe Powers can use some womanly charm."

Powers gave him a tired smile.

"Maybe we'll just have to depend on getting a break, sir."

"Speaking of breaks," Halderman said quietly. "Detective Sonny Breaks is working an undercover operation."

Halderman made air quotes at *undercover*.

"I'm afraid to ask," Gleason said.

"Nothing dangerous," Halderman said. "There's been a number of reports on articles being stolen from cars parked in a private lot in town. Smartphones, laptops, even women's purses, if you can believe someone would leave her purse. No smash-ins or jimmied door locks. We suspect someone at the lot is involved."

"So how does Sonny fit in?" Gleason asked.

139

"Couple of officers have been parking their cars in the lot off and on. Leaving some stuff in sight. Breaks is the detective in charge."

"I thought he was a lifer with the juvenile crimes," Gleason said.

"The decision was beyond my pay-grade," Halderman told him. "What about the bars you were going to check out regarding Meadow? Anything new on Duvall?"

Gleason and Powers exchanged looks.

"Marathon took priority, sir," Powers said. "We'll hit the bars tonight."

Halderman nodded.

"Good. Maybe you'll find something."

"Waste of time, LT," Gleason shrugged, turning for the door. "Been there, done that. But if you insist."

"Wasn't that being a little insubordinate of you?" Powers asked when they'd gotten to their desks.

"What? Laying it out as it is?"

"Not saying you weren't right, sir. But he *is* the boss."

"Ah, yeah, maybe I was kind of flip with him," Gleason said. "He'll get over it. What time do you want to meet for our night out?"

"Probably better earlier than later. Bartenders will have more time to talk before they get busy."

"Okay, you can park near my place and we'll start from there. Head down Duvall to the Pier House and then come back up the other side of the street. Same as before, huh?"

Powers firmed her lips in determination.

"You were absolutely right back there, sir," she said. "It *is* a waste of time. Look, there are a couple of bars in the shopping centers near where I live. Be easy for me to stop by on my way home. Then we'll have covered the entire island. That ought to make the LT happy."

Gleason thought it over for a moment.

"I was hoping to get in a run after work," he said. "Sure you don't mind?"

"Not at all. Enjoy your run. See you tomorrow."

Chapter 29

Jack had stopped by CVS and picked up a copy of *Yachting* magazine. He'd felt a little foolish about buying it but so what? He was just having fun. Not every day you become a yacht owner.

Bobby Sunshine had promised to get a price for the boatyard work within the next couple of days. Jack remembered someone once saying that having a boat was like owning a bottomless money pit. Guess he'd soon find out, he thought, flipping through the magazine.

His cellphone rang.

"Where are you?" Powers asked immediately.

"Home."

"I'll be there in a couple of minutes."

Twenty minutes later she pulled up in front, beeped the horn and rolled down her window. Jack came out on the porch.

"Get in," she called. "I'm taking you on a ride-along."

"Do I need to put on something dressier?" he asked.

He was wearing the standard tee shirt, shorts and flipflops.

"You're perfect. Let's go."

Jack slid into the passenger seat. Powers turned the car around and drove off toward Truman Avenue. She looked over to Jack and smiled.

"I've got to check out a few bars on North Roosevelt. Pass around Lee Meadow's picture and see if anyone knew him. Thought afterwards you could take me to that dinner you promised."

"I like the way you think," Jack said.

~~~

Jimmy Pucket was surprised to see the ProTow yard gates standing open. He figured the boss would've gone home by now. Jimmy had been delayed at his last towing call and it was well after the time when they would've shut down for the day.

He pulled into the yard and stopped to check with the office. A bigger surprise waited inside.

~~~

"I still don't understand why you didn't report it," Powers said to Jack, while waiting for the traffic light to change. "It was a hit-and-run. That's a crime."

"There was nothing to report then," Jack answered. "Everything was a blur. I wasn't even sure what had happened."

"What about the witness?"

"Chuck Banks? Same thing with him. He yelled 'watch out'. A second later, I was flat on my back. I mean, everything happened so quickly."

"But now you believe Candace Farrow was the driver."

"Yes. For all the reasons I said. And don't forget about Matt Wilson, either."

"Right, he's the foggy fellow according to Billy, who remembers cars with his initials on them. You could probably take that all the way to the Supreme Court."

"He's sharper than people think, Rachel."

"Well, maybe I'll pay Candace another visit tomorrow. Here's the bar I want to see."

She pulled into the lot. Only one other car was parked there.

"Interesting name," Jack said, getting out. "*Vanilla*. Ice cream shop?"

Powers laughed.

"I didn't even know it was here until just the other day when I drove past," she said. "You're right about the name but I don't think so."

Inside was almost as empty as the parking lot. A single person sat at the end of the bar picking on a guitar. To her surprise, Powers recognized him.

"Jay Wallace," she said. "We met at the Naval Officers Club."

"Hey, I remember you. Army, right?"

"Yes, you introduced me to that colonel. I didn't know you were a musician."

142

"Just something I do for my own pleasure," he said, going behind the bar and placing the guitar on some wall hooks. "Not in a band or anything like that. What can I get you folks?"

"Oh, you work here now?" Powers asked. "What about the club?"

"This is my second job. I'm still at the club. You know the old saying. Plenty of jobs in Key West. People have two or three of them."

"Jay tends bar at the air station officers club ," Powers explained to Jack.

"Pleased to meet you, Jay. I'm Jack Hunter."

"Is this place new?" Powers asked.

"Been open a little over three months. I fill in two nights a week."

"Curious name for a bar," Jack said. "Why would they call it that?"

"It's an inside joke," Jay laughed.

"I don't get it."

"This is a leather bar," Jay said. "Well, more like kid-leather. Got a softer edge with a cool vibe everyone seems to like. Vanilla is what they call people who aren't into the community. Owner figured the name would be good for laughs."

"I know what vanilla means," Powers said, "but I wasn't sure it had to do with this place. The reason I stopped by is to ask if you recognize this person."

She took out Lee Meadow's photograph from her purse and handed it to him.

"Isn't that the guy who drowned?" he asked. "Saw it in the paper."

He examined the picture more closely.

"Wait a minute," he said. "I think I've seen him in here. Yeah, he was here with another couple and a lady not long after this place opened. I remember now because of how much they ignored the poor guy. He just sat there and nursed his drink while everyone else was having a ball. In fact, he finally got up and left. And you know what? I don't believe they even realized he was gone."

"The others he was with," Powers said, "do you remember anything about them you could tell me?"

"They all came in together," Jay said. "One of the women seemed to be with the drowned guy. What was his name?"

"Lee Meadow. If I brought you a photograph of the woman you believe was with him, do you think you could recognize her?"

"I don't know," Jay said with a shake of his head. "I remember him because I felt sorry for him. I kind of think she was blonde. Not bad looking. She and the other woman were about the same age."

"How about the other man?" Powers asked.

"Seemed like a nice-enough guy. Came off kind of like a smooth operator. Oh, yeah, he left me a good tip. You always remember that."

Powers smiled.

"Did they ever come back?" she asked.

"Not when I was working. You could ask the regular bartender. Name's Terry. She'll be here tomorrow."

"You've been a tremendous help, Jay," Powers said. "Really appreciate it."

A woman entered the bar and sat a couple of seats down from them.

"Hi, Karen," Jay greeted and put a cocktail napkin on the bar in front of her.

"I know you," Jack said, looking over to her. "You took care of me at the clinic. Had a bike accident and hurt my shoulder. I'm Jack Hunter."

"Sorry," Karen smiled. "I'm afraid I don't remember but that's okay. We see a lot of people there. Anyway, how's the shoulder?"

"Doing fine, thanks. Frozen peas did the job."

"They never fail," Karen said.

"Oh, this is my friend, Rachel Powers," Jack said to her.

"Hi, Rachel, I'm Karen Phillips."

"Nice to meet you," Powers said. "I wonder if you could help me with something?"

"You'll have to come to the clinic," Karen joked. "I'm off duty now."

Powers laughed.

"Actually, it concerns this man," she said, showing Karen the photograph. "Lee Meadow."

"What about him?" Karen replied suspiciously.

"It's okay, Karen," Jay broke in. "She's with the police. Good person. I've already talked with her about Lee."

Karen shrugged.

"I'm a detective with the Key West department," Powers said. "We're looking into the gentleman's death."

"I thought it was an accident," Karen said. "Why are the police involved?"

"We're investigating it from a different angle."

"Well, I wouldn't call him a gentleman, if that helps," Karen said.

"So, what would you call him?"

"A fake."

"How do you mean?"

Karen curiously appraised Powers.

"Do you know what the name of this bar means?" she asked. "I'm not talking milkshakes."

"I know what vanilla means, Karen."

"Good, now you know what Lee Meadow was."

"Kind of strange he'd want to hang out here then," Powers said.

"Not if you're a guy who gets his jollies from beating up on women."

Powers let that settle for a moment.

"I've worked with people in the B.D.S.M. community," she said. "And I know the difference between consent and abuse. Are you a friend of Candace Farrow?"

Karen hesitated to answer.

"I've also spoken with Candace, so don't worry that you might say something out of school," Powers assured her. "I have it on good authority that Lee slapped her around. I don't believe it was consensual. Did she ever talk with you about their relationship?"

"Since you know so much about the community, then you must know that some people outside of it consider it illegal, no matter what. Especially the law. Like you."

"I'm only interested in Lee Meadow," Powers said.

Karen nodded.

"Yeah, we did talk about it. Candace can be a little paranoid but not about Lee."

"What about Candace's other friends? Were they as perceptive about Lee as you?"

"Her main buds were," Karen said. "The three of them were tight. But they knew each other long before Lee came on the scene."

"It'd be great if I could speak with them," Powers said. "Would you mind giving me their names?"

Karen sighed.

"I don't know if I should," she said.

"I certainly wouldn't ask you to do anything that you don't feel right about. We just want to get this thing settled so everyone can go about their business. It'd be a big help but do what you have to do."

Powers looked her in the eyes, a sympathetic smile on her lips.

"Okay," Karen said. "Just don't let them know I told you. It's Amanda and Drake Boynton. I think they live in Casa Marina."

~~~

Stock Island Sheriff's station answered the 911 call, a possible homicide at a local towing company in the area.

A deputy arrived at the scene to find a dead man lying on his side behind the desk inside the office at the vehicle impound yard. A chair was overturned, and the desktop computer monitor had been knocked over. Other items were scattered about, all indicating a possible struggle had taken place. The victim had apparently suffered a chest wound. A gun lay on the floor near him.

The deputy immediately called his sergeant, explained the situation and requested detectives be sent. He then took charge of the person who'd phoned in the 911.

Within minutes, another Sheriffs car had pulled up, followed shortly by the lead homicide investigators. He went over the scene, careful to disturb nothing, then called for the deputy in charge of documenting, who commandeered the entire office. No one else was allowed to remain there while he worked. For all practicality, he owned it until he was satisfied everything had been covered. He used a simple digital camera, one without photo manipulating capabilities to head off any questions concerning authenticity that might arise later on. After he had finished, the scene was given back to the lead homicide detective who once more examined the victim in situ. He put the gun in an evidence bag and gave the okay for coroners to come.

The man who'd phoned in the 911 still waited anxiously with a deputy. The lead detective went out to talk with him.

"I'm Sheriff's Detective George Ashby," he said. "How're you doing, sir?"

"Kinda still shook up," Jimmy Pucket answered with a weak smile.

"Don't blame you," Ashby smiled back. "Pretty shocking thing to walk into. Like to ask you a couple of questions."

"Yes, sir."

"Run me through what happened," Ashby said. "From the time you got here until you called us. I know you've already spoken with the deputies, but I'd like to hear it myself."

"Like I said, the gate was open and I pulled in the yard. Funny thing was the office door was standing wide open, too. Frank keeps it shut."

"That's the man who was shot," Ashby interrupted.

"Yes, sir. Frank DeSilva. He's my boss. Anyway, I went inside, and he was laying there on the floor. I took one look and called you guys."

"Do you know if he kept a gun?" Ashby asked.

"Sure did. Big-ass automatic. Had it in the desk drawer."

"What about money? Much cash around?"

"Sometimes," Pucket said. "It depended on the time of day. Frank liked cash better than credit cards."

Could be a robbery gone wrong, Ashby thought to himself. An opportunity for anyone who knew about the money.

"Any other employees than you, Mister Pucket?" he asked.

"No, just myself. We've only been here for a couple of months. Frank was thinking of getting another driver."

"He interview anyone lately?"

"Never said anything to me. He'd have to run it past the owners before hiring anybody. They're in Miami."

"Let me ask you this," Ashby said. "I would imagine some people get pretty upset when they come here to get their car back. Any of them ever threaten you or Mr. DeSilva?"

"No, they just blow off a lot of steam and then pay the bill. I don't blame them for getting mad. I'd be pissed, too. But then they either parked where they shouldn't have or stayed too long, right?"

"Can't argue with that," Ashby said. "So, there's no incident that stands out from the others, that what you're saying?"

Pucket thought for a moment.

"Don't know if this matters or not," he said, "but the other day I brought in a Land Rover. Frank joked about how the two ladies it belonged to had raised hell over it being towed when they came to get it. Claimed I'd taken the wrong car. People try anything, you know? Anyway, earlier today, I passed that same Land Rover coming this way just as I was about to get on the highway."

"Are you sure it was the same vehicle?"

"Yes, sir, I remember it had a vanity license plate. Bunch of letters. Probably in the computer."

Pucket indicated toward the office.

"Thank you, sir," Ashby said. "You're free to leave. Anything come up we need you for, we'll be in touch."

He watched Pucket go to his car and then went back inside the office. The computer monitor was lying on the desk. He didn't touch it but instead phoned for the Sheriffs technical squad.

~~~

"There's a La Trattoria by the airport," Jack said. "Want to try it?"

"Sounds good to me," Powers said.

She joined the traffic on North Roosevelt Boulevard, which switched to South past Houseboat Row, and soon they'd parked in the lot by the restaurant. They were shown to a table and a waiter immediately greeted them.

148

"Hi, Chuck," Jack said. "Didn't know you worked out here."

"Filling in," Chuck Banks told him. "One of the waiters is out sick. Some kind of flu going around."

"Chuck's the gentleman who helped me after the accident," Jack explained to Powers.

"Glad to meet you, Chuck. I'm Rachel Powers. Jack said you saw the car that hit him, is that right?"

"I just saw a blur. Lucky we both weren't killed."

"Do you think it was intentional?" Powers asked.

"Probably just a crazy driver," Chuck shrugged. "Can I get you something from the bar?"

"We'll take a look at the wine list," Jack said. "Give us a minute."

"I haven't had a chance to talk with your neighbor," Powers said, after Chuck had left the table. "You still believe she ran into you?"

"Yeah, I do. Just don't know why."

"Well, it might be tough to prove she was the driver without a witness."

"What about Matt Wilson?"

"Too vague, Jack."

This wasn't what Jack wanted to hear but he realized she was right.

"Well, vague or not," he said, "I believe him."

Powers smiled.

"And I believe you believe him," she said.

"That woman we talked with at the bar?" he said. "I'd seen her once before. I was out for an early morning walk. Sun hadn't even come up. She was getting out of a car. She was dressed like a nurse only it was more of a costume. Kind of over the top."

"Maybe she was returning from one of her role-playing games," Powers said. "What's the point?"

"I just thought it was interesting, that's all," Jack said, examining the wine list. "There's a nice merlot here. Billy has had it at the restaurant a couple of times."

"Good enough endorsement for me."

Jack ordered the wine. They split an order of fettuccini between them and ended with a couple of expressos.

"I could fall asleep right here," Powers said.

"Be better if we went home to a warm bed." Jack suggested.

"Yes, but I'm too tired for anything other than sleeping."

"Sometimes just being close is enough."

"That's a sweet thought."

~~~

"Drake, come quick," Amanda called from the den.

Drake was busy in the kitchen. The chocolate soufflé, his specialty, was due out of the oven now and not a minute later.

"You've got to see this," she called again, a note of urgency this time.

He could hear the television blabbing insanely. What on earth could be that important to drag him away? She knows you can't interrupt a soufflé.

"It's about that awful towing man!" she shouted.

He flung open the oven door, whipped out the soufflé and plopped it down on the kitchen island.

"What the hell are you talking about?" he said, rushing into the den.

"He's been murdered," Amanda said, pointing at the tv screen.

Drake sank into a chair. The soufflé fell in the kitchen.

~~~

Across town, Candace was watching the same news program in her living room, a smirk on her face. The little bastard probably stiffed the wrong person, she thought.

"The victim was identified as Frank DeSilva," the reporter at the scene stated gravely. "He was the manager of the towing company."

"Were there any other people involved?" the news anchor asked, the screen splitting the picture to include him at the studio.

"An employee discovered the body," the reporter answered.

"Do they have any suspects," the news anchor jumped in. "Any sign that this could be a terrorist act?"

150

"At this point, the Sheriff's department is treating it as a suspicious death. That's all I have."

Candace turned off the tv. She wondered if Drake and Amanda had seen it? Maybe she should drive over there. They could celebrate at Vanilla. She grabbed up her car keys and left.

~~~

Amanda scraped the ruined soufflé into the garbage disposal. Drake sat on a chair at the kitchen island.

"He was all right when I left," he said.

"Why did you even go there?" Amanda asked, stacking the pan in the dish washer. "Sure, he ripped us off but it was over. You couldn't have done anything about getting our money back. So, once again, why did you go?"

"It's a long story."

"Well, I'd like to hear it."

The doorbell rang.

"I'll get it," Drake said, grateful for the interruption.

Candace rushed in as soon as he opened the door.

"Did you see the news?" she asked excitedly.

"Is that you, Candace?" Amanda called out. "I'm in the kitchen. Drake was about to tell me a fascinating story. Come on back and we'll have a glass of wine."

Chapter 30

Gleason had doubled down on his runs. He'd done six miles the night before and another six this morning. Now he was at his desk reading the crime reports. A homicide on Stock Island headed the list. Apparently happened yesterday afternoon. The Sheriffs had picked it up. One of their detectives was an occasional running partner. He decided to give him a call.

"Sheriff's Department, this is Deputy George Ashby."

"George, Earl Gleason here. Just reading about that 782 out on Stock Island yesterday."

Seven-Eighty-Two was the Florida statute on murder.

"Yeah, possible robbery gone bad is the way I see it," Ashby said. "Victim was a manager at a new towing outfit that'd set up shop near Cow Key. Word is he kept a lot of cash around."

"Pretty isolated location," Gleason said. "Anyone see anything?"

"Tow truck driver thinks he might've. He found the body. How're things there?"

"Staying busy," Gleason said. "Look, if there's anything you need from us, give a shout, okay?"

"I'll do that. Still putting in the miles?"

"Last night and this morning. Six by six. Join me the next time. If you think you can keep up."

"You'll be surprised," Ashby said. "Say, I've gotta go. Good talking with you, Earl."

Powers came in just as he ended the call.

"Good morning, sir," she said. "Had coffee yet?"

"Just about to go for a cup. How'd your barhopping turn out last night?"

"Very interesting."

After returning with their coffees, Powers filled him in on her visit to Vanilla.

153

"I bet the two people Karen Phillips mentioned as being Candace Farrow's best friends are the same ones Jack saw her with at Louie's," she said. "Sure left there in a big hurry. Wonder why?"

"Yeah, they could be," Gleason agreed. "But when you think about it, how big a deal is that? I mean, the fact they ran out. Maybe the woman can't stand being around Hunter, decided to simply leave. Can't say I blame her."

"I know you have a problem with Jack Hunter, sir," Powers told him, "but I believe there was more to it than her just not standing to be around him. If not then, certainly now."

Gleason leaned back in his chair.

"Okay, I'm listening."

Powers took a breath. She could be about to make a fool of herself.

"The other day, Jack was knocked off his bicycle in a hit-and-run incident."

"Was he hurt?" Gleason asked.

"Nothing broken. Just bruised shoulder where the right-hand mirror clipped him. There was a witness, but it all happened too quick. Couldn't ID the car."

"Did he report it?"

"No, but he began to remember a few things. He believes it was a dark blue car. According to another witness, a dark blue car was seen speeding near the scene. He identified it as a blue BMW. Candace Farrow owns a blue BMW and Jack saw it at a repair shop with a broken right-hand mirror. He took a picture of it. I realize this is all circumstantial, but you can't just ignore it."

"Everything about this case is circumstantial, far-fetched, paranormal," Gleason said after a moment. "Might as well add one more piece to the pile. Boy, would I welcome some solid evidence."

Powers smiled.

"I think we should talk to the Boyntons, sir."

"Whatshername at the bar didn't give you their address, did she?"

"No, but it shouldn't take too long to find it. Want to call first or drop by and say we were in the neighborhood?"

154

"Rude works better."

~~~

There'd been no celebration at Vanilla the night before. After Candace arrived and Drake had explained why he'd gone to the impound yard, a shouting match had erupted with finger pointing all around. During a heated moment Drake had inadvertently dropped a bombshell on Amanda. He'd let slip the reason behind his concern over the missing windscreen. Then everything came out. Toothpaste would've been easier to squeeze back in its tube, a cat more than willing to return to the bag. Now at ten o'clock in the morning, the three of them sat quietly on the patio by the pool.

"There's nothing to worry about," Drake said wearily, breaking the silence. "The more I think about it, I doubt if anyone would even know what the thing is. Much less where it came from."

"That's not the point," Amanda said. "Why didn't you tell me what had happened at the beginning? Both of you keeping something like that to yourselves is simply unimaginable."

She gave Candace a stern look.

"Don't you realize how serious this is?" she continued. "You could go to prison. Or worse. This is Florida, don't forget. And now you've involved me! I can't believe it!"

"I'm sorry," Candace said tearfully.

"If we'd put our heads together back then," Amanda sniffled, "maybe we could've figured out something better. Isn't that what we've always done?"

Drake reached across the table and took her hand in his.

"You're right," he said. "We panicked and did something stupid. We just didn't want to involve you."

Candace placed her hands over theirs.

"Friends take care of friends," she said in a shaky voice.

"You know, if Candace hadn't stepped in when she did, I might not be here," Drake said, a catch in his voice now. "Maybe both of us would be dead or certainly injured. He was out of his mind."

"Oh, what the hell," Amanda said. "The jerk deserved what he got. I think you're pretty brave. You did what you thought was best."

The land-line phone rang in the kitchen.

"I should've gotten rid of that thing long ago," Drake grumbled, getting up from the table and going inside.

"Hello!" Drake said sharply, grabbing the phone off the receiver.

It'd taken the Sheriffs' in-house hacker less than twenty minutes to get in the ProTow computer. Ashby then had him print out every file. The first one he'd gone to was the towing job listings and the last entry on it was a black Range Rover, Florida license RPLAYR. A quick request to motor vehicles had provided its registered owner and address.

"Good morning, sir," a pleasant voice replied. "I'm Deputy George Ashby with the Monroe County Sheriff's Department. Is this Mr. Drake Boynton?"

Drake felt something jittery pitter-patter through his gut.

"Yes," he answered warily.

"Mr. Boynton, we're conducting an investigation that perhaps you could help us with. It concerns a vehicle registered in your name. Do you own a Range Rover?"

"Uh, yes, but I can't imagine what that would have to do with whatever it is you're investigating?"

"Well, we think it may be pertinent. I wonder if I could come by and speak with you?"

"I'm kind of busy right now," Drake said.

"Shouldn't take long, sir. If you'd rather, we can clear this up at the station."

"No, no, I can make time."

"Very good, sir. I have your address."

Drake put the phone back on the receiver and stood there a moment to sort this out. Why did the Sheriffs want to talk to him? What was it about his car they needed to know? If Amanda hadn't parked in that stupid lot and gotten towed, none of this crap would be happening. He started to return to the patio when the doorbell rang.

"Jesus Christ," he muttered aloud. "Will it never stop?"

"Is that someone at the door?" Amanda asked, having come in from the patio.

"Yes, yes," Drake said exasperatedly. "I'll get it."

"Who was on the phone?"

"J. Edgar Hoover," he snapped.

He fumed all the way to the front door and was surprised to find two people waiting there when he threw it open.

"Mr. Drake Boynton?" Gleason asked, reaching into his pocket for his badge. "I'm Detective..."

"What'd you do, call me from in front of the damn house?" Drake cut him off. "Real cute trick."

"I beg your pardon?"

"Oh, come on in," Drake said impatiently and stood back from the door. "Is she your partner?"

Powers smiled and nodded.

"Sit anywhere you like," Drake said, sweeping a hand toward the living room.

Gleason and Powers sat on the sofa. Boynton took a chair across from them.

"I assume this has to do with that fellow who was killed on Stock Island," Boynton said hurriedly. "Well, like I just told you on the phone, Deputy...er, Ashby, right. I don't know how I can help you. My car was towed out there the other day, if that means anything. Wife was using it and apparently overstayed her time in a parking lot."

Gleason turned to Powers and then back to Boynton.

"The incident on Stock Island belongs to the Sheriff's Department, sir. I'm Detective Earl Gleason and this is Detective Rachel Powers. We are with the Key West Police Department. We're here on another matter."

Drake gave them a blank look as Gleason and Powers showed their badges.

"I thought you were...," Drake began to say in bewilderment. "Never mind, I guess there's been some kind of mix-up."

"We just need a little information, sir," Gleason smiled, removing Lee Meadow's photograph from his coat pocket and placing it on the coffee table. "It shouldn't take long. Do you know this person?"

Drake stared slack-jawed at the photo. Amanda entered the room, Candace a few steps behind.

"Why, Miss Farrow," Powers said, spotting Candace. "What a pleasant surprise."

~~~

"It could've been self-inflicted," Blake Harding noted. "That's just a preliminary observation. Powder burns around the entry wound, which was on left side of the sternum. Bullet exited the back, shattering the left clavicle, indicating an upward trajectory."

Harding was on the phone with George Ashby. The medical examiner had driven down from Marathon first thing this morning to begin the autopsy.

"Yeah, we dug a slug out of the wall," Ashby said. "Large caliber. More than likely came from the weapon we found at the scene. Forensics will confirm it."

"Some suicides shoot themselves in the chest," Blake said. "Can't bear the thought of disfigurement. Exactly where was the bullet you found located?"

"Higher up on the wall than if he'd been in a sitting position. Also, the desk chair had been knocked over and was on the floor. No hole in the back of it. Papers and things scattered. Sure looks like a fight could've taken place."

"Well, if there'd been a struggle for the gun and it went off, that'd be consistent with the wound. There are some bruises and scratch marks on the victim. So they were possibly made pre-mortem."

"The gun's being checked for prints," Ashby said.

~~~

The three of them now sat in the living room with the two detectives, Gleason and Powers seated on the sofa, Amanda and Candace in chairs near Drake. Gleason was doing most of the talking.

Powers studied the group. She remembered Karen at the Vanilla mentioning that the Boyntons and Candace were tight friends but this bunch was like they shared the same brain. It was fascinating to watch. Also, she felt they were lying.

She smiled at Candace and broke in to ask her a question.

"One thing still puzzles me from the last time we spoke. You said you were out of town when Lee Meadow's photograph appeared in the newspaper, is that right?"

"Yes, I didn't learn what'd happened until later," Candace said.

"How about you, sir?" Powers asked Drake and then Amanda. "And you, ma'am, were you both also away?"

Drake and Amanda looked at each other.

"No, I guess we must have just missed seeing it," Drake said. "I don't pay that much attention to the local paper."

Powers nodded. A few seconds of silence followed.

"Well, by the time we found out, everybody knew who he was," Amanda said. "Didn't see what more we could tell you."

Powers turned back to Candace.

"Miss Farrow, you told me that Lee Meadow moved out at your request. There was an issue with him about keeping junk in the yard."

"Yes, he was a packrat," Candace said. "Everything was always in a mess."

"I can understand how that might've upset you," Powers sympathized. "I've seen your home and it's lovely. When we last talked, I believe you said he took the...junk with him? There must've been a ton of it."

"I went out of town after he left. He obviously picked it up then."

"Sure, probably hauled it away himself. He wouldn't have trusted anyone else. And you don't know where he moved?"

"No, as I said, we weren't in touch."

Powers paused for a moment.

"His truck was found in Marathon," she said. "Odd license plate. Whipit. Wonder what that mean, any idea?"

Candace shrugged.

"Anyway, now you know where he moved," she said.

Powers smiled.

"No, I don't think so. In fact, I don't believe he ever left Key West."

Candace shifted nervously as Powers picked up Lee Meadow's photograph from where it rested face-up on some magazines at one end of the coffee table.

"I suspect the truck was there simply to make it look like he did," she said while looking at the picture. "You see, Lee Meadow was already dead when his truck was found in Marathon."

Powers replaced the photograph. The magazine cover caught her attention.

"Only he hadn't drowned," she continued. "He'd been murdered."

The doorbell suddenly rang, startling everyone.

"I'll get it," Drake said, jumping to his feet. Amanda got to hers, too.

In the confusion, Powers grabbed up the photograph and magazine and stuck them in her purse.

"Hold it," Gleason said, putting up his hand, but Drake was already at the door.

A tall man wearing a Sheriffs uniform greeted him.

Chapter 31

Jack had earlier had business at a bank in town and was returning to the parking lot where he'd left his Jeep. The bank had drawn a cashier's check in Bobby Sunshine's name for forty thousand dollars as payment on the *Joyful Noise*. Officially, Jack was now the boat's new owner. Bobby had signed over what papers he had to him. However, he had no intention of keeping it. It was and would always be Bobby's. He'd gone through with the transaction only because Bobby had insisted it be fair and square. As far as he was concerned, he was just holding it for the old guy until he wanted it back. He would run by the house later and give him the check.

Maybe he'd get Bobby to take Rachel and himself on a sunset cruise. Better yet, he would invite her to watch the sunset from the boat while it's tied to the dock. Then, a nice order-in dinner from some place good. Bottle of wine.

He saw a familiar figure lurking behind a large tree up ahead across from the parking lot entrance.

"Detective Sonny Breaks," Jack called out cheerfully.

Breaks snapped his head around, grimaced and put his finger to his lips.

"Shhh!" he hissed and turned his attention back to the lot.

The detective had once taken Jack into custody during a murder investigation without reading him his rights and had been severely reprimanded. The incident had remained a sore spot with him ever since. Jack had brushed it off long ago.

"What's going on?" Jack asked in a hushed voice and peering at the lot himself.

"You're interfering with a sting operation, Hunter," Breaks muttered under his breath. "Move along."

"But my car's in that lot," Jack protested.

"Get the hell out of here!" Breaks shouted.

The parking lot attendant, who was at the back of a van, looked over at them.

"Dammit!" Breaks cursed. "He's spotted me."

Robert Coburn

Breaks charged across the street, waving his badge. Jack watched as he confronted the lot attendant. A scuffle quickly broke out between the two and a wild punch sent Breaks sprawling. The lot attendant took off running directly toward Jack.

Jack stuck out his foot, tripping the man and pitching him headlong onto the sidewalk. Sonny Breaks came up cupping his nose.

~~~

Gleason decided that they'd gotten all they were going to get from the Boyntons and had left the group to the sheriff for the next round.

"I could barely keep from laughing," Gleason chuckled, as they drove back to the police station. "Did you see their faces when Ashby walked in?"

"Cop overload," Powers said. "They'd about reached their limit with us before he showed up."

"I kind of liked that Ashby didn't let on that he knew me," Gleason said. "Interesting ploy."

"Smooth, too," Powers said. "We just made the introductions and no questions asked. Also interesting that Boynton's name has now come up in two homicides. Makes you wonder if there's a connection."

"One thing's for sure," Gleason said. "I'm calling George Ashby soon as he gets back to the station."

Powers reached into her purse.

"Here's something that will absolutely blow you away," she said. "Boynton likes airplanes."

Gleason glanced over to see her holding an aviation magazine.

"It was on the coffee table with Lee Meadow's photograph," she smiled innocently. "I accidentally picked up both of them."

Gleason grinned.

"By accident, huh?" he teased.

"Kind of a special magazine, too," Powers said. "Says it's for aircraft owners and pilots. Since Boynton subscribes to it, he must be one or both."

162

They pulled into the police station lot. Sonny Breaks was just getting out of his car. A large bandage was plastered across his nose. Gleason parked in the spot next to him.

"Looks like someone stuck his nose where he shouldn't have," Gleason said, suppressing a smile.

"My goodness, detective, what happened?" Powers asked.

"Had to take down a suspect," Breaks said. "Goes with the job."

"Guess we should see the other guy, huh?" Gleason wisecracked.

"Well, you can do just that, detective," Breaks said. "He's in lockup. Got him on running a theft ring, resisting arrest and assaulting an officer."

"Outstanding," Gleason said. "I'm impressed. You *did* read him his rights, I take it?"

"Don't be funny," Breaks huffed. "I read 'em twice. When I cuffed him and when patrol arrived. You can check with the officer and also your buddy, Jack Hunter."

"Hunter? What the hell was he doing there?"

"Getting in the way as usual," Breaks said. "I had everything under control until he walked up."

"Are you saying he interfered with the arrest?" Powers asked.

"Not exactly."

"Why don't we go inside and have a cup of coffee," Powers suggested. "This is all very exciting and I'd love to hear all about it."

~~~

Deputy George Ashby warmed the same sofa that Gleason and Powers had earlier shared in the living room at the Boyntons.

Drake Boynton had now recovered from the shock of learning that this was a homicide investigation and was explaining the reason he'd gone to the ProTow lot.

At first, he had been defiant and denied ever having been there at all. Insisted that they must be confusing him with his wife who had indeed been at the lot but on the day before. Ashby told him that he had a witness who'd said otherwise. The witness had identified the vanity license plate on the

Range Rover. And could place him at the scene on the day of the murder.

That last part wasn't exactly the truth but Ashby thought he'd throw it out there anyway.

Drake had stammered a bit and then admitted that, yes, he had been there. But swore to heaven and everyplace else that the man was alive when he'd left.

"I felt the guy shouldn't get away with it," he said. "He ripped off my wife and she probably wasn't the first one. I just didn't like her being taken advantage of."

Amanda smiled sweetly at him.

"The man was extremely rude, too," she said. "I didn't have enough money on me and he was going to charge for another day. Fortunately, Candace came to the rescue."

"Well, rude behavior aside, the tow charges are pretty much standard for around here," Ashby said. "So, in truth, he wasn't ripping her off."

"You've got to be kidding," Boynton laughed harshly. "That's highway robbery and you know it. Also, I bet they've got a cozy setup with the damn parking lot. Probably working together. One or the other could be stealing things out of cars, too. You should be looking into that while you're at it."

"Was something missing from your car, sir?" Ashby asked. "You should file a report."

"I don't leave valuables in my car," Boynton said. "I was just saying it's a possibility."

"Back to when you confronted the man at the impound yard," Ashby said. "What happened?"

"Nothing. We argued back and forth for awhile but I could see it was going nowhere. So I just decided to cut my losses and left."

Ashby raised his eyebrows.

"You simply walked out? After he'd purposely overcharged your wife? I thought you said you weren't going to let him get away with that."

"Well, yeah," Boynton shrugged. "I'd made my point. Besides, it wasn't the money so much as it was the principle."

"The principle?" Ashby smiled quizzically.

"I stood up for what I believed," Boynton said indignantly. "He proved to be a cheater."

"But this man was rude to your wife," Ashby said, turning to Amanda. "Do you share your husband's beliefs, Mrs. Boynton?"

"We both believe in being fair," she said.

"And how about you, ma'am?" Ashby asked Candace. "Go along with that?"

"He was a pig," Candace snapped.

"So, you wouldn't have let him off so easily," he smiled. "Were you there?"

"Absolutely not!" Candace said, raising her voice and glancing at the other two.

"Did the three of you go out to the lot?" he asked. "You were convinced you'd been cheated. The guy was uncooperative. Rude you said. One thing led to another. Tempers flared. Suddenly, it all got out of hand. I can understand how that might've happened."

"This is outrageous," Drake shouted. "I went there alone. The girls knew nothing about it."

"Do you own a gun, Mr. Boynton?" Ashby asked.

The deputy hadn't mentioned how the victim had been killed.

"No, I don't like guns. Actually, I'm afraid of them. I wouldn't keep one in the house."

Ashby looked at him for a moment and then decided he was telling the truth.

"All right, sir, we'll leave it at that for now," he said. "However, there may be questions you can help me with at a later time."

He stood up to leave.

"Just out of curiosity," he said. "The two detectives that were here when I arrived. Had you also made a complaint about the parking lot in town?"

Boynton hesitated before answering.

"No, they were here on another matter. A friend of ours had an accident. Like I said, nothing was taken from my car but now that you mention it, maybe they should look into it. Town doesn't need businesses like that."

"I'll see myself out, Mr. Boynton," Ashby smiled and tipped his hat. "Thank you for your time."

~~~

"Can't find that damn title," Bobby Sunshine said, folding the bank check and sticking it in his shirt pocket. "Looked through everything. Dad must still have it back in Swanquarter. I'll get it to you, though. Joyful Noise is your boat now, fair and square."

Jack had driven to the house on Ashe Street to finalize the deal. Bobby and Roy were at home. Ruth had gone to the gym.

"Don't worry about the title for now," Jack said. "How's your dad doing?"

"He's fine. Be better once he gets that new hip. Already thinking about buying another crabbing boat."

"Sounds like he's in good spirits," Jack said. "Thought it was his knee that was giving him problems. So, it's his hip, then?"

"Did I say knee? One of those joints. I run 'em together sometimes."

Bobby didn't sound right, Jack thought to himself. Something was in the air but he decided not to pursue it.

"When did Ruth start going to the gym?" he asked instead.

"Few days ago," Bobby sighed. "Friend of hers belongs to a group that meets there two or three times a week. Got her to join up."

"Didn't realize Ruth was into fitness," Jack said.

"She's into gossip. All they do is sit on those bicycles that go nowhere and talk. I suppose it's a good thing for right now. I'm thinking of going to Swanquarter to be with my dad. Give her something to do while I'm gone."

"Yeah, your dad would probably like you being around for his operation," Jack said, walking over to Roy who was perched on a lamp.

"And how's my favorite bird?" he asked, smoothing the feathers.

"Ah, he's a lonely little fellow," Bobby told him. "Seems Sebastian has finally flown the coop."

Sebastian was a Key West rooster living rough that'd made their block his home and would exchange crows with

Roy every morning at sunrise. This routine had gone on for several years to the annoyance of everyone within earshot.

"Might've been a contract hit," Jack said.

"The Lord works in mysterious ways," Bobby smiled.

Chapter 32

"I think Detective Sonny Breaks owes you a drink, Jack," Powers said.

She'd called him from the coffee room at the station after hearing about the action at the parking lot.

"Only if you stand in for him," Jack joked.

"I can do that. After work?"

"Be great. How about Mallory Square? "There's a bar on Wall Street with a great salsa band. And we can watch the sunset celebration."

Jack remembered he'd promised himself to take her there after seeing it himself.

"Is there someplace a little less noisy?" Powers asked. "Not that I have anything against salsa. Nor the sunset, for that matter."

Bobby Sunshine's boat came to Jack's mind. Settle in a couple of chairs on the deck with a nice bottle of wine. But, on second thought, having to drive out to Stock Island wasn't all that appealing.

"Tiki Bar at the Galleon," he said instead. "Same sunset from the deck but without the salsa."

"I'll meet you there. Around six?"

Jack said he'd be on time and she ended the call. A crowded bar and an earsplitting salsa band was just what she didn't need. She had to make a decision soon and she needed to talk with him about it. The letter from Fort Benning she'd gotten yesterday was still in her purse. She returned to the detective's room. Gleason was on the phone.

"Hold on a sec, George," he said. "Detective Powers is here. I'm going to put my phone on speaker."

"Hi, George. I'm Rachel."

"Hi, Rachel," a tinny voice said. "Fun and games this morning, huh?"

"We laughed all the way back," Gleason said. "Before you start, let me tell you why we were there. Detective Powers and

169

I are investigating a homicide and it seems that the folks you were visiting are possible persons of interest to us. Go ahead."

"Strange people," Ashby said. "I'll say that much. A Range Rover belonging to Boynton was seen near the impound lot on the day of the crime. It'd been towed there the day before and bailed out by Boynton's wife. At first, Boynton claimed he'd never been to the impound lot. When I told him I had a witness, he admitted he'd gone there to complain about the tow charges his wife had paid. Suggested that the parking lot and tow yard were cohorts in stealing stuff from cars. Backed off that, though. I asked the two women in the house had they gone with him. They denied it. My feeling is they're all in cahoots about something but I'm not sure what. Forensics should have prints on the gun soon. I may be paying the Boyntons another visit then."

"All right, George," Gleason said. "Thanks and good luck."

"What do you make of that, sir?"

"Which part? The cahoots thing?"

"Yes, I think they're definitely hiding something. They were ambiguous in about everything they said. Too bad the sheriff came just as we were getting into the surveillance pictures about the truck."

"We may have to pay them another visit ourselves," Gleason said. "Better make sure we're on solid ground. Boynton could start complaining about police harassment. I'll run it by the Lieutenant."

"Why don't we try to find out more about Boynton's involvement with airplanes first?" Powers suggested. "I could nose around the airport. Remember that man out there who helped us with the Pittway case? What was his name? Oh, yeah, Bob Dean. I'll get in touch with him tomorrow."

"Sounds good. I'm ready to call it a day. You set?"

~~~

Jack found a parking space on Front Street near the Galleon. The Tiki Bar was packed but a couple of stools still remained empty at the rail overlooking the harbor. He grabbed one. A two-masted sailboat slowly passed by in the channel heading for open water, its sails billowing.

He'd never gone on a sunset cruise. He wondered what it was like. A tap on his shoulder brought him out of his thoughts.

"Been waiting long?" Rachel asked.

"Just got here," Jack said, pulling back the other stool. "I was watching that sailboat. We should do that sometime. What would you like to drink?"

"White wine would be nice."

Jack went to the bar. The musician arrived and began to tune up his guitar.

"There's a table on the deck," Rachel said when Jack returned with two glasses of wine.

"Let's take it," Jack said. "Be quieter."

They placed the chairs around to one side so they could face the sun.

"Best show on earth," Jack smiled.

Powers put on her sunglasses.

"Detective Sonny Breaks sends his regards," she said.

"Here's to the detective," Jack replied, clinking his glass with hers. "Anything new with my neighbor?"

"Nothing I can talk about."

Several gulls wheeled in the air scanning the water.

"But there is something we need to talk about," Powers continued.

"That sounds serious. Is it?"

Powers took a sip from her glass.

"The other organization I work for wants me full time," she said.

"I'm not sure I understand."

"The United States Army, Jack. They're short of people in my specialty."

"You mean they're recalling you? I thought they only did that in time of war."

"Well, there're a lot of wars going on but no, I'm not being recalled. It's just they've made me a pretty nice offer and I'm not sure about what to do."

"What did they say?" Jack asked.

"You know I just made captain in the reserves. They'll fast-track me on the major list if I go regular. That would be a big deal. I'm talking career."

"But what about here? I mean, your job with the police? I think that's kind of a big deal. Sounds like a career to me."

Powers sighed and shook her head.

"It is, Jack. Well, in a way. Sure, I enjoy what I'm doing. It's just I'm not certain about the future. Key West is a small department. Not a whole lot of options when you come down to it."

She dabbed at her eye.

"The head of homicide may be retiring next year. I'm not supposed to know but Gleason told me. The lieutenant asked him to take the exam. Said he'd put him in for the job. But Gleason's being kind of willy-nilly. So I don't know what the hell is going to happen."

"What about you?" Jack asked. "Did the lieutenant offer the job to you?"

"Gleason's been with the department longer."

"Doesn't matter. You're just as qualified. Maybe better considering your military experience. He still could've at least offered. Where would you be posted if you take the Army deal?"

"I'd probably go to Fort Benning. At least at first. It's in Georgia."

"That's not so far," Jack smiled. "Georgia's only a short hop from here."

"I know what you're thinking," Powers said. "That could work for now but who knows where I might be sent later? Europe? Africa? Back to the Middle East? It just doesn't seem fair to you."

"I don't care about what's fair, Rachel. I'm glad for what we have right now. I want you to be happy. How long before you have to give them an answer?"

"They recently sent me a letter. I have to make up my mind soon."

"Then give it the thought it deserves. Be honest. And whatever you decide, I'm with it all the way."

"Can we get out of here?" Powers asked. "I hate to be a spoilsport but right now I'm not in a party mood."

Jack stood and pulled out Rachel's chair for her. His eye fell on a biplane flying a few thousand feet above Christmas Island. As he watched, it rolled upside down, held that position for a moment and then turned upright again.

"Boy, you better remember to fasten your seatbelt when you fly in that thing," Jack commented.

Powers looked at him in astonishment.

"What did you just say?"

"What?"

"About that airplane."

"Don't fly upside down without a seatbelt," he laughed.

She gave him a big kiss.

"Now, *I* owe you a drink, Jack."

~~~

Sheriff George Ashby was at his desk in the Stock Island Sheriff's Station, the sun having taken a final bow at Mallory Square hours ago.

While pouring over the file printouts from Frank DeSilva's computer, he'd come across a job application. It'd been the last item in the bunch and kind of sad, he'd thought. The name on it was Richard Elliott and listed his address as being in Big Pine. He was a truck driver. Poor guy probably lost his job and house in the hurricane. Obviously, they hadn't hired him here. The application was a month old.

Ashby rubbed his eyes and checked his watch. He put the stack of paper in the desk drawer and flicked off the lamp. It'd been a long day.

Chapter 33

"You're saying that the seatbelt is the only thing keeping you from falling out," Powers said.

She was on the phone speaking with a pilot who worked at Bird's Eye Views, an aerial sightseeing company at the Key West airport. The man who'd helped her in the Pittway homicide was no longer at the flight operation company she'd originally called but another person there had put her on to the touring outfit. It was still early in the day.

"Absolutely," the man confirmed. "If the airplane has an open cockpit and you're upside down, you better be belted in or hold on tight. Or hope your parachute works."

"Tell me a little more about the airplanes you use," Powers said.

"We have a Stearman. That's an old military trainer. They've been around forever. Ours has been rebuilt, of course. We use it for short hops around the island. Kind of just chugs along. People like it. Seats a passenger up front. Pilot flies from the rear cockpit."

"Can it turn upside down?"

"You could do a slow roll but if you're looking for a real thrill ride, you'd want to take our Pitts for a spin. Literally. It's smaller than the Stearman and fully aerobatic. Does loops, Cuban Eights, snap rolls, and like I said, spins."

"I don't know what those other things are but you *are* saying the planes can fly upside down," Powers pressed for confirmation.

"Upside down and right side up. They're happy either way."

"You mentioned that passengers sit up front in the first plane," Powers said. "Is it the same with the Pitts?"

"Both are biplanes. Means they have two wings, one on top and one on the bottom. Two cockpits, one behind the other. Stearman's an open cockpit. The Pitts has a full canopy. You still need to fasten your seatbelt though."

"I'd like to see those airplanes," Powers said. "Okay if I come by?"

"Sure, we're next door to the terminal. I have a flight scheduled in the Stearman about an hour from now. Should be free after that."

"I'll see you then. Thanks."

She hung up and grinned at Gleason, who was sitting across from her.

"I think it's at least plausible," she said. "I haven't given up on the idea that Meadow could've been kicked out of a large airplane, but this is starting to look good."

"Just imagining it gives me the willies," Gleason said. "They would've had to load the body in that plane before it took off. Then he's just sitting there the whole while flying along until he's dropped out. Talk about macabre. Something else, too. Sheriffs crime lab has finished with that shot of Meadow's truck by the parking lot. Might have to drive up there. Said it'd be better to look at it on a large screen."

"How about showing it on a movie screen?" Powers asked. "Take it to the Tropicana."

"I asked them that. They laughed. Said I had to be kidding."

"Wait a minute, sir," Powers said. "They meant a monitor screen. You've got one in your apartment. That obscenely huge high-definition television set."

"Christ, why didn't they say so?"

~~~

Sheriff George Ashby had also heard from the crime lab. The prints found on the Colt .45 used in the DeSilva homicide had been identified. It was a familiar name. He sent out a call for the man to be brought in.

~~~

Jack had taken Bobby Sunshine to the airport and stopped back by the house afterwards to visit with Ruth.

"His plane get off alright?" Ruth asked.

They were in the kitchen.

"As far as I know," Jack said. "Hope his dad's knee operation goes well."

"It's not his knee. It's his prostate."

176

"Prostate? Why did he say it was the knee?"

"Embarrassing subject. I finally got it out of him."

Jack shook his head in disbelief.

"He's also worried it might run in the family."

"Does Bobby get regular checkups?"

"Too embarrassed."

"Well, that's just crazy."

"Bobby left this for you."

She handed Jack the title to *A Joyful Noise*.

~~~

The idea of viewing the security camera pictures on Gleason's monster television set in the comfort of his apartment didn't fly. It'd be a nightmare to pull off, he had been told by someone knowledgeable in technology. Also, questions about transmitting possible evidence to a private residence had been raised as a final nail. Gleason was skeptical about that last reason, but he decided not to fight it. The detectives would just have to drive to the Sheriffs crime lab.

"I promised that guy at the airport I'd see him and it's almost time now," Powers said. "Shouldn't take long. We can make the lab this afternoon."

"How about we split up?" Gleason suggested. "You go to the airport and I'll do the crime lab. You okay with that?"

"Shucks, I really wanted to see those pictures on the big screen," Powers said.

"If there's anything important, I'll have the techs make prints. Think they should be able to do that."

"All right, sir. I'll see you back here."

Chapter 34

Powers held the shoulder straps with both hands in a death grip while looking up at the Gulf of Mexico passing below. Her body strained against the seat belt. She pressed her feet to the floor to keep her legs from banging into the instrument panel. Gravity changed and pulled her back into the seat as the airplane slowly rolled upright again. It was exhilarating and frightening at the same time. And more importantly, told her what she'd wanted to know.

"How was that?" the pilot's voice crackled in her headset.

"Can we do it once more?" she asked, wondering how smart it was to have gotten herself into this but nonetheless determined to see it through. "And this time stay upside down a little longer?"

"Roger."

The horizon quickly rotated clockwise in the windscreen and stopped sharply at six o'clock, the clouds below, the water above. Gravity tugged at her with full force. There was no way she could've remained in the airplane without the seat belt and shoulder harness tightly fastened.

"Good enough?" the pilot asked. "I can hold it a little longer if you want."

Powers grunted that it was enough, and the airplane snapped upright and began a slow turn toward the island.

"Ready to return to the airport, ma'am?"

"Roger," Powers squeaked, unable to resist the term.

"Let me show you a loop first."

~ ~ ~

Sheriff's deputies spotted Richard Elliott in front of his home in Big Pine. They were able to pick him up without incident. Had he been inside the house, they'd have needed a warrant. He now sat alone in an interview room at the Stock Island station.

"He give you any trouble?" George Ashby asked, viewing Elliot on the console screen.

179

"No, sir," the deputy answered. "We told him he was needed at the station and he was fine with it. Just wanted to know if we'd give him a ride back home."

"Amazing," Ashby said.

He opened the door and entered the room. Elliot stood up.

"Have a seat, sir," Ashby said. "I'm Sheriff's Detective George Ashby. How are you today?"

"I'm all right. Just curious about why you wanted to see me."

"I can understand that, sir. And I'll get right to it. But first, I have to confirm that you are Richard Elliott. That true?"

"Been called that all my life," Elliott said with a nervous little laugh. "Guess it must be true."

Ashby returned a smile.

"Mr. Elliott, the reason we asked you to come in has to do with a homicide investigation. Now, I'm going to read you your rights to protect both of us."

Elliott remained silent while he was being Mirandized.

"Do I need a lawyer?" he asked when Ashby finished.

"That's entirely up to you, sir. Do you want a lawyer?"

Elliott heaved a breath.

"No, go ahead," he said.

"Mr. Elliott, do you know a man named Frank DeSilva?"

Elliott made a puzzled face.

"Maybe this will help. You filled out a job application for him at ProTow."

"Yeah, now I remember," Elliott said brightly. "Hell, that was so long ago I'd forgotten."

"Actually, it was last month. Did he offer you the job?"

"No, I called him a couple of times, but he was always too busy to talk."

"That must've been exasperating," Ashby said.

"I even turned down another job waiting for him to make up his damn mind," Elliott said bitterly. "Somebody else got that one."

"So what happened when you went out there?" Ashby asked quietly.

Elliott didn't answer.

"Mr. Elliott?"

Elliott just stared back.

"Here's the situation, sir," Ashby said. "Mr. DeSilva was found shot to death in his office. We have the gun that was used, and it has your fingerprints on it. So, what happened?"

"Maybe I should have a lawyer."

"Absolutely," Ashby said, getting to his feet. "Richard Elliott, I'm arresting you on suspicion of murder. I'm going to go over your rights again. I want to make sure you understand so pay attention. Anything you say may be used against you in court. If you don't have an attorney, the court will provide you with one. That's the basics. Got it? Now what about that lawyer?"

"Oh, the hell with it," Elliott said. "I haven't got the money to hire a lawyer and what kind of one are they going to give me? I might as well tell you. Get it over with."

Ashby sat back down.

"Yeah, I went there to have a face-to -face with DeSilva. I just wanted to know why he'd kept me on the string if he had someone else in mind. Right away, he gets all pissy and the next thing I know he's grabbed this fucking gun out of his desk and stuck it in my face. I thought he was going to shoot me so I grabbed hold of his hand to get the gun away. We started struggling and it fired. I didn't mean for him to get hurt. I was scared. I just ran."

Ashby gave a sad nod of his head. It wasn't the first time he'd heard a story like that, and it wouldn't be the last time either. He knocked on the door and a deputy came in to take Richard Elliott to a holding cell.

"Will you call my wife and tell her where I am?" Elliott asked him.

~~~

It was late afternoon when Gleason rolled in. Powers was at her desk in the detective's room.

"Traffic's murder today," Gleason said. "Cars stacked up all the way down the Keys. Anything going on in town?"

"Nothing I know about," Powers said. "So...how were the movies?"

"No popcorn," Gleason grinned.

"C'mon, sir, don't keep me in suspense," Powers said.

181

"You were right about having the parking lot scene enlarged. There was a little more picture on the edges of the frame but nothing that would've helped. The lab isolated the truck and blew up that scene. You can see another vehicle pull up and stop but that's about all. The truck has it pretty much blocked. From what you can see, it looks like a sedan. License plate's obscured. Now, here's the real interesting part. The interior light in the truck turned on when its driver got out. And the one inside the car came on when its passenger door was opened to get in. I believe it was a woman who drove the truck."

"Could you see her face?" Powers asked.

"No, she never turned toward the camera. I had the lab make prints of that part. They're not bad. You can take a look."

"What about enhancing software?" Powers asked. "I read that stuff can work wonders in bringing out detail."

"They used all the bells and whistles they have," Gleason said. "There was just not enough there."

"Well, a woman having driven the truck is not bad," Powers said. "Makes me think of you know who."

"Yeah, my thoughts are headed in that direction, too," Gleason said. "Now, what'd your pilot friend tell you about his airplanes?"

"He did better than tell me, he showed me."

~~~

"Have you seen my magazine anywhere?" Drake Boynton called.

He was stretched out on the bed in his shorts. Amanda was in the adjoining dressing room changing clothes.

"Which magazine?" she asked, stepping into the bedroom, nude and holding a dress in her hand.

"The aviation one. There were a couple of articles I wanted to read and now I can't find the damn thing."

"Probably where you left it," she said. "Frankly, I'm more worried about that sheriff."

Drake bristled.

"There's fuck-all to worry about, Amanda," he snapped. "I told you the idiot at the tow yard was okay when I left. And as far as those other two detective bozos go, they're just wasting their time. They have absolutely nothing, believe me."

"I do believe you, darling. It's just the police aren't always as honest as they pretend to be. You read about people being sent to prison for something they didn't do all the time."

"Well, that's not going to happen to me," Drake smiled. "Sorry I was rude just now."

"I rather enjoyed it," Amanda said. "What do you think of this for our dinner date tonight?"

She held up the slinky black dress and shimmied behind it.

"Don't wear anything underneath," Drake grinned.

~~~

Gleason and Powers had updated Halderman on both of their findings and were still in the lieutenant's office.

"That's pretty imaginative detective work, Rachel," Halderman said. "I'm not sure the department will reimburse you, however."

Powers shrugged.

"Their call, sir."

"How much was it again?"

"Hundred fifty. The pilot gave me a break. Normally, it'd been a hundred more."

"Well, I'll see what I can do," Halderman said. "No promises, okay?"

Powers nodded yes.

"I think it was worth every nickel, LT," Gleason protested. "The department damn well ought to pay her back. Now we have a good idea about how Lee Meadow was dropped. At least a reasonable one."

"I agree, Earl," Halderman said. "I'm with you both on this. But it's the budget. Money's tight. I'm getting flack about overtime as it is. Can you imagine how they'd look at this thing? It'd just be a joyride in an airplane to them."

"City Hall," Gleason muttered with a shake of his head. "Anyway, that's where we are, LT. Try to run down some airplane owners in the area tomorrow. Probably will take a warrant."

"Do what you have to do," Halderman said, dismissing them with a wave of his hand. "Good work, the both of you."

The two detectives left the office and walked out to the parking lot.

"If you ever needed a reason not to become part of the brass in this department, there was one," Gleason grumbled.

"I feel sorry for the lieutenant," Powers said. "He's over a barrel."

"Well, that's just it, Rachel. The number crunchers always run the show. I'd go crazy if I had Halderman's job."

"No, I think you'd make it work, sir. Same as he does."

~~~

Gleason relaxed with a glass of wine on the front porch at Vinos. He'd driven home, fed the cat, put together a makeshift dinner for himself from leftovers in the refrigerator and afterwards had decided to walk over to Duval Street.

The last light of day dawdled in the western sky as a few stars began making their distant appearance in the east.

Powers' comment about the job was on his mind. He probably could run homicide. Make it work, as she'd put it. The question was did he want to? Right now, he was happy with what he was doing. Sure, it was frustrating having to fight his own people upstairs, but he could get around that. The truth was he liked the action on the street. Pushing paper just wasn't in him.

Still, he had to look at his future. That sheriff's deputy who was about to retire came to mind. The guy had a lock on what's ahead for him. Cushy job waiting with a big security company. Probably a hell of a lot more money, too. Not a bad life. What's he got in store for himself? Say twenty years from now?

He gave a sarcastic laugh. They'd probably have kicked him out long before then.

So where will he be when he decides to pull the pin? Realistically. A used-up homicide detective hoping to find a job pounding the beat at a shopping center? Or instead perhaps a captain. Or even better. And with options.

Traffic had picked up on the street. Lots of monotonous thump-thumps booming from the radios in the passing cars and trucks. Pedestrians shuffled along the sidewalks. Three men standing in front of Vinos began arguing noisily among themselves in a fusion of angry words and bad language. It sounded as if a fight might break out any minute.

Gleason got up and leaned over the porch rail.

"Hey, you three down there!" he shouted in his fiercest command voice. "That foul language isn't allowed here. Shut up and move on!"

They did.

Gleason sat back down, a little smile creeping across his face. How could he even think of ever giving this up? He finished his glass of wine and left.

Chapter 35

"**T**urn off the water," Amanda shouted urgently. "Candace just called."

"Oh, God, is she still pissed because she wasn't invited last night?" Drake replied from inside the shower stall. "I thought I'd explained that the party was a business thing. She wouldn't have known anyone there."

He stepped out and grabbed a towel off the rack.

"They've arrested someone for killing that awful man," Amanda said excitedly. "It's in the paper."

~~~

"Congratulations," Gleason said over the phone. "Just finished reading the story in this morning's rag. Nice work."

He was at his desk, having gotten in early. Powers hadn't arrived yet. In fact, he was the only one there.

"Thanks, Earl," George Ashby said. "How's it going with that case you're working?"

"Inching through the swamp but I think we're getting there. Actually, I was surprised to read about this Elliott person. When you showed up at the Boyntons, I thought one them might've been your prime suspect."

"Tell you the truth, I was angling for Drake Boynton but evidence proved otherwise. Boynton was telling the truth all along."

"Well, once again, good work, George. Take care."

"Hey, Earl, before you go, a few of us are going for a practice run today at noon around the air station at Boca Chica. You up for it? Going to be a fast run."

"Navy let you do that?"

"Not officially but a commander there is a runner. Been out with us a couple of times. He said things are quiet since most of the jets are up in Pensacola readying for fun and games with the fleet."

"I'm in."

Powers entered the room just as Gleason hung up.

"You see the morning paper, sir?" she asked, holding up a copy.

"I was just talking with George Ashby over at the Sheriffs about that. He and some others are having a run at Boca Chica around lunchtime. Think I'll joint them."

"Have fun," Powers said. "The good thing about the Sheriffs arrest is that it leaves Drake Boynton to us. You want a coffee?"

"You sit," Gleason said. "I'll get it this time."

A couple minutes later he returned with two cups of coffee and a grin on his face.

"Just ran into Sonny Breaks," Gleason chuckled. "Not a happy camper. Apparently that parking lot bust netted a ton of stolen property stashed in the perp's van. Breaks is stuck with cataloging all of it."

"Why's he doing it?" Powers asked. "Thought that was Thompson's job."

"He's out sick today," Gleason said.

"Well, maybe it'll keep Detective Breaks off the streets for a while."

"How do you want to handle this airplane owner thing?" Gleason asked. "First, how many hangers are we looking at?"

"I don't know. Ten? Twenty? However, many they have at the airport."

Gleason laughed.

"Do we have probable cause for even one?" he asked.

"I was thinking of just asking around," Powers said. "If someone gets uptight and demands a warrant, then we'll talk to the judge."

"He won't sign one for a fishing expedition," Gleason said.

"Maybe it'll never come to that," Powers smiled. "I'll do a test run and call our friend at the Marathon airport. Good place to start anyway."

"Turn on the charm," Gleason laughed. "I gotta go see what's going on with Breaks in the evidence room. This is too good to miss. Be back in a minute."

~~~

Jack watched the *Joyful Noise* make its way to the channel. He'd contracted with a boatyard farther up the Keys to have it hauled out. They had sent a captain down to bring it up.

Bobby Sunshine had made a list of repairs that needed to be made. Jack had decided not to wait for him to return but instead go ahead and get the work done now. He'd figured one less supervisor would be much easier on everyone in the long run.

He had earlier considered moving the boat back to the Key West Bight, thinking the location would be more convenient than Stock Island. But that idea had stirred up a bad memory. It'd been at the Bight and while he was living aboard her that he'd narrowly escaped from being murdered. Stock Island was a perfectly fine berth.

The *Joyful Noise* rounded a point of land and disappeared from view. Jack stood at the empty slip. His life could possibly take a new turn, too. He wondered where it would lead.

~~~

Gleason had come back on the double to get Powers and now both of them were with Sonny Breaks in the evidence room.

"And you were wearing gloves when you took it out of the bag?" Powers asked.

She was looking at what appeared to be a windshield of some kind with a piece broken off the top.

"Yes, detective, I was wearing gloves," Breaks said wearily. "I know the procedure for handling evidence."

Powers smiled.

"I didn't mean to imply that you didn't, Sonny. Just that this could be really important if it's what we think it is."

"Lucky I got here when I did," Gleason said. "I couldn't believe it when I saw this thing. It's like what you'd described from your airplane ride, Rachel. This could be from a plane."

"Yeah, well, it looks more like a windshield from a motor scooter, if you ask me," Breaks shrugged. "Why would anyone even want it? Easier just to buy a new one than try to glue it back together."

"That the bag it was in?" Gleason asked, pointing to a large trash bag on the table.

"Yeah, I'd just taken it out when you came in," Breaks said. "Had to see what it was so I could enter it in the computer. Bad enough to have to haul all this junk in from the van without having to catalog every damn piece. Hope Thompson's enjoying his day off."

"The poor guy's home sick in bed," Gleason reminded him. "Bug going around. I had it myself. Surprised you haven't caught it yet."

"Whatever," Breaks said. "You want me to stick the thing back in the trash bag?"

"No, see if there's some paper bags around here big enough to hold it and put the trash bag in a separate one," Gleason said. "Might be forensic evidence on the windshield. Could be prints inside the plastic one so be careful how you handle it."

While Breaks went to search for something suitable, Powers took several photographs of the windshield with her cellphone.

"I don't think it came off a motor scooter," Gleason said. "Well, not off of any I've seen."

"Think this'll work?" Breaks called out, holding up a large paper shopping bag from the back of the room.

"Perfect," Gleason said. "Let me sign a release for both and we're out of here."

~~~

A celebratory mood filled the Boyntons' house.

"You know, I've a good mind to call that damn sheriff," Drake said. "Tell him a thing or two. Barging into our house and practically accusing us of murder. Makes you wonder about the kind of people they hire."

"Oh, that awful man isn't worth the bother, Drake," Amanda said. "They've arrested someone and we're none for the worse. But you're right, it was upsetting at the time. And as far as the person who was killed on Stock Island goes, he probably deserved what happened. It was just karma catching up."

"We should go out tonight," Drake suggested. "How about Vanilla? Call Candace. She'd love it."

"That's a wonderful idea," Amanda beamed.

"I haven't flown the Great Lakes in forever," Drake mused. "Maybe I'll grab some time. Fly up to Marathon this afternoon."

~~~

Gleason and Powers were going through the murder book for the Lee Meadow homicide.

"That's what I'm talking about," Gleason said, pointing to a photograph mounted on a page. "Remember Harding showing us that sliver he'd taken from Meadow's arm?"

The picture had been taken by the crime lab and was now entered in the murder book.

"Let's get this windscreen to the lab."

Powers frowned.

"I'm worried that there might not be enough forensic material left for the technician to test," she said. "The plastic bag could've degraded what little there was. I know what you said about possible prints being on the inside but everybody and his brother has handled it."

Gleason shrugged.

"Maybe they can tell if our sliver came from the windshield," he said.

Gleason's cellphone sang. He saw it was a call from George Ashby.

"Hey, Earl," Ashby said, "just heard from our mutual friend, Drake Boynton. He was in an uproar over police harassment. Said we should learn to do our job better. I thanked him for his input, and he hung up on me."

Apparently, Amanda's words hadn't soothed Drake.

"He should be relieved he's off the hook," Gleason said. "Sounds like some politicians I know."

"Oh, he mentioned you and your partner. You might be getting a call next. Wanted to give you a heads-up."

"I'll look forward to that," Gleason said. "Be sure to also thank him for his input, too. You ready to go?"

"Yeah, I'm leaving the office now," Ashby said. "See you out there."

Gleason turned to Powers after ending the call.

"I should be back in an hour or so," he told her.

"Like I said, have fun. I'll be here."

After Gleason left, Powers had continued reading through the murder book, again starting with the first entry and paging on to where they now stood. It was frustrating. She closed the binder and sat back in her chair. They'd collected page after page of loose ends but nothing to tie them together.

She took a break and went to the coffee machine.

The windscreen was promising, she thought. She took out her cellphone and looked at the photos of it. Something was familiar. Then it came to her and she felt like smacking herself in the head.

She rushed back to the detective's room, pulled open her desk drawer and grabbed out the aviation magazine she'd picked up at the Boyntons. She'd put it in there after they'd returned and then completely forgotten about it. On its cover was the airplane featured in that issue, a Great Lakes. She quickly thumbed to the article. There were numerous photographs, including a close up of its two open cockpits. And mounted in front of each was an exact duplicate of the windscreen taken from the evidence room.

~~~

Drake Boynton rolled the biplane out of the hanger. It was a whole lot easier job with the little electric tug doing the work. Pulling that old Cessna he'd once owned in and out by hand with only a tow bar took real effort.

He'd already completed a preflight inspection while the plane was inside the hanger. It felt a little strange lowering himself into the seat. He was glad that he had ordered the front cockpit cover to seal it off.

He started the engine and called the tower for taxi clearance.

~~~

The little group of runners was approaching Old State Road 4A on the Atlantic side of the Naval Air Station. It had been a fast pace from the start and Gleason, now feeling the burn, was bringing up the rear. He wanted to save any kick for the last mile, but he couldn't afford to fall too far behind. He picked it up a bit.

Focusing on closing the gap, he never saw the slight dip in the road. He misstepped and his right ankle rolled to send him tumbling. Fortunately, he landed on the soft berm instead of the pavement, but the run was over for him.

Chapter 36

Of course he wouldn't have his cellphone on him, Powers thought, as her call went to voicemail again. It was probably left with his clothes since he would've changed to a running outfit. But shouldn't he be finished by now? She decided not to leave another message.

Is everyone not answering the phone today, she wondered. She'd called the air tour company only to find no one there. Same thing at the Marathon airport. She'd dutifully left messages at both places to please call her. It was exasperating.

She saw that Halderman had finally come in and was at his desk. She decided not to wait any longer for Gleason to show up. She'd tell the lieutenant what they'd discovered and discuss their next steps.

Her cellphone chimed right then. She saw it was Gleason.

"Did you get my message, sir?" she answered anxiously. "I think I have the name of the airplane. I mean, what kind it is."

"I'm in the emergency room at the hospital," Gleason said. "I turned my damn ankle. Probably a bad sprain is all. George Ashby's here. What's this about the airplane?"

Powers filled him in. Insisted that there was no doubt in her mind that the windscreens matched.

"Outstanding, Rachel," Gleason said. "Is the lieutenant there?"

"Sitting in his office. Want him to call you?"

"Let me find out what's going on here with the doctor first."

"Okay, call me as soon as you know more."

~~~

"That a new Great Lakes?" Clayton Hawkins asked.

"Less than fifty hours on the clock," Drake Boynton answered proudly.

Hawkins had spotted the trim little biplane sitting on the tarmac in the transient parking area and had walked out to it

195

for a better look. Boynton was conducting a cursory preflight before flying back to Key West.

"Always loved that airplane," Hawkins said. "Years back I went through a basic aerobatics course in one. Nothing like swooping around the sky in an open cockpit."

"Thought that was for the birds," Boynton joked.

"What made you get a Great Lakes?"

"Friend took me up in one a few times. Found out I liked it. Later on, I decided why not get an aerobatic airplane. Sold my Cessna and bought this."

"Looks like we might be getting some weather," Hawkins noted, scanning the darkening sky. "What's the forecast for Key West?"

"It was clear when I left. I can beat this back to the airport."

Hawkins shook his head.

"Why don't you wait it out here," he offered. "Stuff comes in awfully fast. We can put your plane in the hanger if you're worried about it."

"Thanks, but I have to get back."

~ ~ ~

Gleason had gotten bad news on top of bad news. Along with having sprained his ankle, he'd also fractured his fifth metatarsal. He decided to call Halderman first instead of Powers.

"It's one of the long bones in your foot," he explained. "Connects to the little piggy."

"Do you have a cast on it?" the lieutenant asked.

"No, it's a hairline fracture. It'll heal itself. The doctor gave me a boot to wear. I can take that off and soak my foot in ice water for the ankle."

"How long before it's well?

"The doctor mentioned six weeks but he's just being super cautious. You know how they are. I'll be in tomorrow."

Halderman looked out into the detective's room. Powers was busy at her desk. Sonny Breaks came in carrying a cup of coffee.

"No, Earl, I think it'd be better if you took off a few days," he said. "Get some rest."

"But Rachel and I are getting close on the Meadow homicide," Gleason protested.

"Detective Breaks is free. He can help Powers."

"He'll only screw everything up," Gleason said. "At least run it past Rachel, okay? She should have a say."

Halderman considered that for a moment.

"All right, I'll talk with her before I decide. And I mean that about taking some time off."

As soon as Gleason hung up, he dialed Powers. She answered on the first ring.

"What did you find out, sir?" she asked.

"Bad news. The lieutenant might stick you with Sonny Breaks."

Powers laughed aloud.

"I cracked a bone in my foot," Gleason continued. "Minor stuff but Halderman wants me to stay home for a few days. He wants Sonny to work with you until I'm back. I asked him to speak with you first. But I've a feeling he's already made up his mind."

"Are you serious?"

"Yes. I just got off the phone with him."

She looked over at Halderman's office. It was empty.

"I think he's gone to the restroom," she said.

"Now's your chance. Run for your life."

"Call me later," Powers said, gathering up her things and heading out the door.

~~~

Visibility worsened by the minute and rain had begun to fall. Drake Boynton squinted through the windscreen. There wasn't much he could see straight ahead. He'd hugged the line of keys since leaving Marathon, keeping them in sight so he would have some sort of orientation. The airplane wasn't instrument equipped, which really didn't matter since he wasn't rated to fly by instruments.

His altimeter indicated nine hundred feet. He nudged the control stick forward and descended another hundred. He also turned more to the east. He figured he was about twenty miles out of Key West airport. Turbulence suddenly jolted the little airplane. Rain pelted down even harder and the sky darkened.

There must be another storm cell hidden in clouds, he thought. He should've listened to that guy at Marathon.

The Cudjoe Key tethered balloon radar system, affectionately known as *Fat Albert*, commanded the airspace up to 14,000 feet within a radius of 3 miles of its mooring platform. A strong steel cable held the balloon place. The restricted area was 17 miles from Key West airport.

Drake was relieved to see solid ground below him again. At least now he had reference and could tell he was flying level. He grabbed another quick look at the altimeter which indicated he was now at only seven hundred feet. He never saw the cable looming ahead of him.

~~~

Air Force, Navy, Coast Guard, Homeland Security, FAA, FCC...the list went on and on concerning the number of agencies overseeing the Aerostat balloon. Since the accident was an aviation incident, the FAA would undertake the initial investigation. Monroe Country Sheriffs, however, were the first responders to the crash site. And for the moment, they were in charge.

"Earl, I don't suppose you've heard about that airplane accident up near Cudjoe Key," George Ashby said. "But before I get to that, though, how's the ankle? I hated to leave you at the hospital, but I had to go to the Stock Island marina. Guy set off an alarm. Deputies answered and found him hiding in an unlocked shipping container. He lived there as well. Ran him and he has several warrants in Ohio for dealing in child pornography."

Gleason was at home sitting out on the deck. The rain had finally ended and had left Key West clear and clean.

"Glad you got that scum off the street," Gleason said. "Foot's feeling fine. Might be that the pain medicine hasn't worn off yet, but I can get around pretty good with the boot the doctor gave me. In fact, I drove home. Now, what's that about an airplane accident?"

"Private plane flew into Fat Albert's tether during the storm. Witness heard the crash and called us. Pretty bad. Pilot was killed. I went there after the marina business and that's why I'm calling you. It was Drake Boynton. I recognized him but we'll have to confirm his prints."

"Holy Smoke, was he the only one aboard?"

"Yes. Don't know how this affects your investigation but thought you should know right away. Soon as we get the confirmation, we'll notify the family. Should have that within the hour."

"How'd he manage to fly into that thing? The balloon's location been marked for years on every chart available."

"My guess is he got lost and strayed over to the cable's location," Ashby said. "Shouldn't have been flying in that weather. Anyway, he smacked into the cable and lost control. Apparently, he wasn't very high. Witness said he heard the engine and it sounded like the plane was low right before the crash. No fire, thank goodness. It's a wonder that the cable didn't break."

"Well, thanks for calling, George. Yeah, this is definitely going to affect our investigation."

This Meadow homicide case was beginning to rank up there with the strangest ones he'd ever worked on. What could happen next he was almost afraid to think.

~~~

Powers had gone straight home. She realized that she couldn't avoid the lieutenant forever but she only needed a little time to collect herself. The idea of having to work with Sonny Breaks was simply impossible. She'd made a cup of tea and was standing in the kitchen considering calling Jack. Maybe having a strong shoulder to cry on tonight would be nice. Her cellphone rang. She saw it was Gleason.

"Hello, sir, do we need a secret code to talk?"

"You aren't going to believe this," Gleason said, ignoring her joke. "Drake Boynton has been killed in an airplane accident. Just heard the news from George Ashby. Happened up in Cudjoe Key."

She sat down.

"What do we do now?" she asked. "This is devastating."

"I think we should continue with the investigation," Gleason said. "There are still the two women. I believe they were all three involved."

"It's so incredible," Powers said, still stunned, "for this to have happened. I just don't know what else to say. And now here you are with a broken foot. Is this whole case jinxed?"

Gleason laughed that off, although he'd been thinking the same thing.

"Nothing to worry about," he said. "I'm going into the office tomorrow. We can work together there and stay in touch by phone when you're out. You okay with that?"

"You bet. But what about Sonny Breaks?"

"Forget him," Gleason said breezily. "He could only be a gofer at best. Otherwise you're inviting disaster. The lieutenant knows that. Say, how about using your boyfriend for a gofer? Slightly better choice than Breaks."

"That would be all right with me, but wouldn't it need some kind of official authorization?"

"It's not like we need to deputize him or anything. Like I said, he'd be your gofer."

"You could tell the lieutenant that Jack actually did go on a ride-along with me recently," Powers suggested. "Believe it or not, he was helpful."

"I'll take care of the lieutenant," Gleason said. "Just keep Hunter on a short leash."

~~~

Amanda Boynton's emotions zigzagged between concern and anger. Drake should've been back from Marathon long ago. She'd reasoned that the storm may have delayed him. But wouldn't he have at least called to say he'd be late? He knew they'd made plans for evening. Candace was due there any minute. Still, she couldn't help but worry. She hated that damn airplane! Should she turn on the news? No, she was too afraid.

The doorbell chimed. It must be Candace, she thought with relief. At least now she'd have company to share in the misery.

"It's open, sweetie," she shouted.

Another ring accompanied by a knock this time.

Amanda threw up her hands in exasperation and went to open the door. Two uniformed Sheriff's deputies with solemn expressions stood there.

"Is this the residence of Drake Boynton?" one of them asked.

"Yes, what is this about?"

"And are you a family member of his?"

She sensed something dark and foreboding was about to step through the doorway.

"I am his wife," she said apprehensively.

"May we come in, ma'am?"

Chapter 37

Powers had phoned Jack after speaking with Gleason and then had driven to his house to further explain what his role would be, providing Halderman agreed to go along with the idea.

"It's not that I don't think you're capable, Jack. "Actually, I'm pleased Detective Gleason suggested you. It's just we can't afford any mistakes. I don't want to give some clever defense lawyer a gift."

"You're the boss," Jack said.

"I'm serious," Powers said firmly. "At any point where evidence is involved or we're in contact with a potential witness, let me handle it. Say nothing, touch nothing, stay out of the way. This is different from the time we went to that leather bar."

Jack smiled.

"I've got it," he said. "Now, when do we start?"

"We start by having a nice dinner somewhere."

That was also what Candace had in mind for tonight at Vanilla with Drake and Amanda as she drove past Jack's house on her way to theirs. She noticed the car parked in front. Probably belongs to the cop bitch, she thought. She took another look at her watch. She hoped they'd forgive her for being so late. That awful storm had threatened to flood the lane. There'd been nothing to do but wait for it to stop raining.

~~~

The house had grown dark and she should turn on some lights, Amanda thought. But somehow the darkness seemed almost palliative. She sat on the bed in the stillness.

After the deputies had left, and for no particular reason, she'd gone up to the bedroom and rummaged through Drake's clothes hanging in the closet. She had even taken down a favorite jacket – a light worsted wool blazer – and pressed it to her face, feeling its texture and taking in its scent.

All of this will have to go, she'd thought sadly. Clothes. Shoes. His stuff. She could call a charity and they'd come for them, she supposed. Not everything, of course. She'd keep a few reminders.

It wasn't like he'd moved out; they'd gotten a divorce or something. She could've accepted that. It would've been civilized for one thing and for another there would've been time. Time to get used to the idea. But this. Dear God, he was here this morning!

She got up from the bed and walked over to the window. The patio lights had automatically turned on, as if in readiness for the two of them to come down for a glass of wine. Funny, she hadn't cried yet.

There are arrangements to make, she thought. A funeral to plan. And where would that be held? Drake wasn't from Key West. What little family he had was somewhere in one of those ocean-less states. He'd been estranged before they'd even met. The deputies said she would be notified when his body could be released. Would she have to go pick it up herself? She'd never been through anything like this.

It occurred to her that while Drake was gone, life goes on. All the things he took care of – paying the bills, house upkeep – they were now her responsibility. And what about their income? Would that change? How did he get paid anyway? She should have been more involved in their finances. She suddenly felt helpless. Damn that stupid airplane! Damn him for doing this to her!

The doorbell chimed cheerfully from downstairs.

She took a deep breath and went to answer it. She suspected she knew who was there. A smile creased her face.

Chapter 38

Gleason had slept fitfully with his foot out from under the covers and resting on the floor. As long as he didn't put any weight on it, he was comfortable. Mitts was up and about, however, and meowing for breakfast.

Expecting a jab of pain, he gritted his teeth and chanced to stand. He felt confident enough to hobble to the kitchen, where he shook out two pain tablets that'd been prescribed and downed them with a glass of water. Then he fed the cat.

He'd better get himself together, he thought, if he's going into the station.

Powers had no intention of showing up there herself. She was driving to the Key West airport. Jack followed in his Jeep.

She had decided they shouldn't ride together. She realized it was silly and of no consequence but despite Gleason's assurances, she still had misgivings. This crackpot idea of subbing a civilian for a sworn officer wasn't even on the protocol map.

The airplane crash on Cudjoe Key had headlined the morning paper. She had phoned Clayton Hawkins at the Marathon airport and had learned that he had spoken with the pilot and that the airplane was a new Great Lakes. Hawkins also said he'd warned him about the developing thunderstorm and had suggested he wait it out there. He said he believed the man hadn't had much experience with weather.

Powers pulled into a space in the airport parking lot. The Jeep took the one next to her.

"I'll just introduce you as my friend," she said to Jack, as they walked toward the general aviation area. "I don't want them to think you're also a cop. In fact, I'd like to keep this whole thing low-key."

"How about I say I'm interested in taking an airplane ride?" Jack offered.

"Don't say anything."

Powers had earlier found that the pilot she'd flown with at Bird's Eye Views had taken the day off, but another person had agreed to see her. They entered the small office. A man sat at a desk.

"Hi, I'm Rachel Powers. Are you the gentleman I spoke with earlier?"

"Bill Watson," he said, standing up.

He looked at Jack.

"I'm Jack Hunter. Just a friend."

"Too bad about that accident," Watson said. "Doesn't pay to mess with Mother Nature."

"Did you know the pilot?" Powers asked.

"Not personally as a friend but we're a small family at the airport."

"Well, I'm interested in finding out more about his airplane," Powers said, taking out her cellphone and scrolling to a photograph. "We believe this is an airplane windshield. Could you tell what kind of airplane it came from?"

Watson examined the picture.

"Obviously it would've been an open cockpit," he said. "Could possibly belong to a Great Lakes. Tell you what. Like me get our A&E mechanic. He'll know."

Watson picked up the phone and called. A few moments later, the aircraft and engine mechanic entered the office.

"Charlie, the lady here has a question for you," Watson said, foregoing any introduction.

"Hi, I'm with the Key West police department," Powers said, showing him her ID and then the photo. "Do you recognize this?"

Charlie shook his head sadly.

"Guess it doesn't matter now," he said. "That looks like the windscreen I took off of Drake Boynton's Great Lakes. He didn't want me to tell anyone."

"You're certain of that?" she asked. "It belonged to his plane."

"I'd have to see the one you took the picture of," Charlie said. "yeah, I'm ninety-nine percent sure. Boynton said a friend had accidentally broken it while bracing himself getting into the cockpit. Guy must've been pretty clumsy is all I can say. Anyway, I replaced the windscreen and left the damaged one in the hangar for him."

"And when was that?" Powers asked.

Charlie thought for a moment.

"Not sure exactly," he said. "I do a lot of maintenance work for different owners here. Have to check the airplane's maintenance log."

"Do you have it here?"

"No, he kept that in the hangar. We can run down there. I have a key."

~~~

Amanda and Candace were on the patio having coffee. They'd talked well into the night and Candace had decided to stay over rather than drive home. The sunny morning promised a beautiful day.

"Drake was going to call someone about that pool," Amanda said wistfully, noticing a few bubbles gurgling on the surface of the tiny pool.

"I just wish we could go back to the way it used to be," Candace said. "Before all this other mess started. We used to have so much fun. Now everything's changed. It's so ironic to think I was coming here last night to tell you both about passing the realtors test and I should soon have my license."

"That's wonderful news, honey," Amanda said. "I know you'll be a success."

"What are you going to do about the house?" Candace asked.

"Why, I hadn't thought about that," Amanda said in surprise. "There's been so much to take in."

"I was just curious. It's kind of big, is all."

"Well, when I decide, I'll let you know," Amanda said coolly. "Funny, I halfway expect Drake to walk out and join us any minute."

"I know. We were always together in everything. The three musketeers, he used to call us, remember?"

"We still have each other, sweetie," Amanda said, reaching over and patting Candace's hand. "Drake would never want that to change."

Candace frowned.

"Lee could change it," she said uneasily. "Those cops aren't going to quit their stupid investigation just because of what happened to Drake. They're suspicious enough already. That'll probably make them look all the harder. In fact, I saw that police cow's car parked at her lover's house when I left last night. I know he's spying on me for her."

Amanda put the empty coffee cups on a tray and stood.

"Drake must've driven the Range Rover to the airport," she said. "I should go get it. Will you drive me there?"

~~~

"You're supposed to be off-duty today," Halderman said. "Why aren't you at home?"

The lieutenant had just returned from an early meeting with the chief and had spotted Gleason sitting at his desk.

"I'm fine. Easier to keep tabs on things here than at home."

"Where's Powers?"

"Boynton crashing his airplane and killing himself has kind of complicated things. She's following through on that. We'll stay in touch by phone."

"Well, Sonny Breaks can partner with her," Halderman said. "I'll assign him to the case when he comes in."

"That's really not necessary, Lieutenant. Like I said, we've got it worked out."

Halderman pulled a chair up to Gleason and sat down.

"Look, Earl," he said quietly, "I understand where you're coming from but suppose Powers needs someone. Breaks is all I have at the moment."

He stood to leave.

"And suppose you need a detective available to answer a call?" Gleason countered. "Like you just said, Breaks is all you have. You don't want to get caught short. I'm riding the desk. Powers has all the help she needs."

"All right, all right, you win," Halderman said and returned to his office.

Gleason let out a breath. Better not to mention anything about that help being Jack Hunter.

~~~

The aircraft mechanic opened the side door and flicked on the lights. He'd driven Rachel and Jack to the hangar in a golf cart.

"Logbook's in the desk," he said. "I'll get it."

"Wait, let me go with you," Powers said. "Jack, would you mind staying here? Just for a minute."

"Kind of dark even with the lights on," Charlie said. "I can open the hangar door if you want."

"That's a good idea," Powers agreed.

Charlie hit a switch and the door rumbled up and stopped overhead. He and Powers walked to the back of the hangar.

"What's that thing?" she asked, pointing at a metal bar with a tee-shaped handle on one end leaning against the wall.

"Tow bar," Charlie said. "You use it to move the airplane around. Usually it's kept in the airplane. Guess he wanted to save space."

The tee-shaped handle caught her interest. She looked at it more closely. Then she took out her cellphone and scrolled to the picture she'd taken of the wound on the back of Lee Meadow's head the day his body had been found on the beach.

"Don't open the desk, sir," she said urgently. "We both need to leave."

"Thought you wanted to see the log," Charlie said, slightly confused. "Okay, I'll close the hangar door."

"No, leave it open and don't touch anything else," Powers told him. "Call airport security to send someone here, then I'd like you to take my friend back to your office. As of now this building is a possible crime scene."

She thought now she'd better get a warrant.

Chapter 39

The Key West airport security had assigned a man to secure the area until a police crime team arrived. Once it was on the scene and Powers had explained the situation, the first step had been to completely document the hangar interior with both photographs and video. After that forensics had taken charge.

A luminal test had quickly confirmed a suspicious stain on the floor toward the rear of the hanger to be blood. The tow bar's handle had also appeared to contain traces of blood and possible tissue. It would be sent to the lab.

The aircraft's maintenance log and everything else inside the desk, including Boyntons' pilot log, had been collected as evidence.

"I have a question," Powers said to one of the forensics technicians. "We believe the body was placed in an airplane. Would there still be any viable DNA in the plane?"

"Possibly. It could be recovered from a surface that the skin touched. We call that 'touch DNA'. Problem is it's kind of a crapshoot because it's not visible, so you just have to hope it's there when you swab the spot."

Powers nodded.

"Suppose the airplane had crashed and had been outside before you could get to it?"

The technician laughed.

"Then the hope factor goes up, up and away."

~ ~ ~

Candace had circled the airport parking lot twice before they found the Range Rover. She pulled in next to it.

"Oh, damn, I forgot to pick up the extra set of keys," Amanda said. "I feel so stupid. Now we'll have to go back."

"It's all right, sweetie," Candace smiled. "You have a lot on your mind."

211

"Let's just sit here for a moment," Amanda said. "I was thinking over what you said about the police becoming a bigger problem."

"I'm sure they know more than they're admitting," Candace fretted angrily. "That's how they trick you into saying something you shouldn't."

"Well, Drake might be able to help us with that."

"Honey, I realize you're in shock but Drake's no longer around."

"Exactly the point," Amanda said. "I could tell the police that Drake confessed to me. He said that they had a fight at the hangar and Lee fell and struck his head. Drake panicked and got rid of the body."

"Do you think they'll believe that?" Candace asked.

"Why not? It's close enough to the truth. They'll probably be glad it's over."

"But won't they want to know why you didn't tell them sooner?"

"He told me the day he had that terrible accident, honey, right before he went to the airport. That was the first I'd heard of it. Said he'd been trying to protect me, but he couldn't keep it in any longer."

"That is so like Drake," Candace said dreamily. "One for all and all for one."

"And just to back him up, you were with me when he said it."

~~~

Gleason sat at his desk in the detective's room with his foot comfortably propped on an overturned wastebasket. Powers had phoned to update him on what they'd found at the hangar.

"I believe Lee Meadow was killed here, sir. There are blood stains on the floor. Someone tried to wipe them up but missed a spot under a bench. We may have the murder weapon; something called a tow bar. Also, the airplane's maintenance book has an entry in it for a windscreen replacement. Even better, we have the person who did the work."

Gleason looked toward Halderman's office in hope of catching the lieutenant's eye so he could motion for him to come over, but the room was empty. He checked his watch.

"How long before you're finished there?" he asked.

"We're about to wrap things up now. Should I come in?"

"No, I think the lieutenant's gone for the day. Think I'll split, too. We can fill him in tomorrow."

"There's one more thing, sir. I had this idea that there might be some DNA evidence in Boynton's airplane. I asked the tech about it and she said it was iffy but possible. Think we could get ahold of the plane?"

That was an interesting twist, Gleason thought.

"Worth a try," he said. "See you in the morning."

~~~

Powers had to put in another thirty minutes before the hanger door was finally locked and sealed with yellow police tape. She bummed a ride with the airport security back to the Bird's Eye Views office and was surprised to find Jack waiting there.

"I didn't mean for you to stay here all afternoon," she said. "You should've gone home."

"Part of the job," he smiled. "What's next, Detective Powers?"

"I'm beat. Think I'll take my own advice and go home."

"It's calamari night at the Inedible Cafe. We can grab an early bite."

"How can a girl resist a line like that?"

~~~

Gleason hadn't made it out the door at the police station. Just as he was about to leave, Sonny Breaks buttonholed him.

"Any news on that motor scooter windshield?" Breaks smirked.

"Nothing yet," Gleason said. "You the night dick?"

Breaks hated the slang term used for the night detective-on-duty.

"I'm on call, if that's what you mean," he said testily.

Gleason grinned.

"Guess you've heard about the lieutenant," Breaks said. "Thinking of taking the exam myself."

"What are you talking about, Sonny?"

"Halderman's pulling the pin. Surprised you didn't know."

Breaks flashed a grin of his own and went to his desk.

~~~

Jack and Rachel had split a calamari sandwich.

"I don't see how he makes any money off these things," Powers said. "They're huge. I can't eat any more."

"We make up the loss on booze," Jack said. "Main thing is it builds good local business. Billy's pretty smart about that. You want a to-go box for the rest?"

"You finish it."

She slid her plate over to Jack.

"You going back to the hangar tomorrow?" Jack asked, demolishing the sandwich in two bites. "I'm available, if you need me."

"Thank you but I think we have all we're going to get from there. It would really be helpful to have the airplane."

"Where is it?" Jack asked.

"I don't know. Where it crashed, I suppose."

"Check with the NTSB for the location," he said.

Powers gave him a puzzled look.

"The National Transportation Safety Bureau," he told her. "They investigate all kinds of accidents."

"Of course, they would be involved," Powers said, mocking a smack to her forehead. "Too focused on one hand to see the other."

"Also, they might've moved the airplane," Jack said. "A guy I knew in Los Angeles ran his airplane through the fence at the runway. Ended up in the middle of a street. They stuck what was left of it in a hangar for the investigation."

"I wonder what happens to the airplane when they've finished?" Powers said.

"Usually, it's returned to the family or the owner. In the guy's case back in LA, it was the bank."

"Jack, you are an absolute wonder, do you know that?"

Chapter 40

Powers had learned from the NTSB watch officer at the bureau's headquarters in Washington D.C. that the Great Lakes had been trucked to a hangar at the Marathon airport because the crash site was in an ecologically sensitive area. The investigation into the cause of the accident hadn't been completed. After some back and forth over the phone with her arguing that the airplane was also considered to be a crime scene and possibly held evidence in a homicide investigation, they'd struck a deal. Apparently, the NTSB needed the deceased pilot's flight log, which was now in the KWPD's possession. Powers agreed to turn over the logbook to them in exchange for permission to examine the wreckage. Just to be safe, she'd armed herself with another search warrant before gathering up a forensic technician and driving to Marathon. Now she'd returned to Key West and was in the detective's room with Gleason.

"On the plus side, most of the interior was painted metal," Powers said. "Having a smooth, non-porous surface was important. The tech swabbed every place in the front cockpit his body might've touched, including the seat."

"Must've been creepy having to look at that plane," Gleason said.

"I've seen creepier. We should have results back from the lab pretty quick. I have my fingers crossed anyway."

"Well, here's already one result that just came in from them," he smiled, clicking the mouse on his computer and swiveling the monitor around so she could see the screen.

Powers slowly read the message.

"Should we pick her up, sir?"

Gleason considered that for a moment.

"The print ID on the tow bar is pretty strong evidence," he said. "It definitely proves she's been at the scene, although, we don't know if it was during the crime. Too bad it's not a bloody fingerprint but, yeah, we could take our chances and go with

221

it. The lab's waiting for the complete forensic test to come in. They went ahead and sent the print info now. Nice of them."

Powers gave a frustrated sigh.

"Christ, there's already so much stuff there begging to be looked at," she said. "Okay, how about this? We give them until tomorrow and if nothing new turns up, we bring in her ass for a little talk."

Before Gleason could answer, his phone rang. He didn't recognize the number.

"Homicide. This is Gleason."

"Detective Gleason," a woman answered. "This is Anne Nilsson with the Ft. Myers crime lab. We've completed the blood and DNA tests on the tow bar. I'm emailing the results to you. I assume you received the fingerprint identification I earlier sent. Somehow your job was kicked up to first in line. Probably a mix-up in priority but lucky for you. Anyway, we're expediting everything as quickly as we can."

"You're an angel, ma'am," Gleason said. "Keep it coming."

~~~

Ft. Myers kept it coming until nearly midnight. When Gleason and Powers did finally leave the station, they had the analysis for every spec of evidence collected from Boynton's hanger. They'd also gotten results back on the aircraft windscreen. Powers had asked if they could expedite the DNA gathered that day from the airplane in Marathon. She was politely told that she was pushing her luck but they'd see.

~~~

"This is absolutely great work," Halderman said.

Gleason and Powers were in the lieutenant's office laying out the results from the crime lab.

"Thank the lab," Gleason said. "They put in the overtime."

"The dimensions of the tow bar handle fit the shape and size of the wound," Powers said. "That and the blood and tissue match leave no question about it being the murder weapon."

"She must've really swung for the bleachers on the guy," Gleason said. "Her prints were like she was gripping a ball bat."

"What time is she coming in?" Halderman asked.

"Should be any minute now," Powers answered. "Both of them are coming. Here's the interesting part. She said they were going to call us. Had something important to tell us."

"We'll let them do the talking first," Gleason said, turning to leave. "Then we'll spring the good stuff."

"I like it," Halderman said. "Earl, stick around for a second."

Powers returned to her desk.

"Just be aware," Halderman said. "Detective Breaks has put in for the lieutenants' exam."

"He mentioned something about doing that," Gleason said.

"We both know that guy has political pull. So, what I'm saying is get those papers in pronto. Take the damn test."

"What about Powers? She'd be good."

"You're my recommendation, Earl. Now, don't keep the ladies waiting."

~~~

Powers led Candace and Amanda to an interview room.

"We'll have more privacy in here," she smiled, opening the door for them. Gleason was already seated at the table.

"Good morning," he greeted.

Candace and Amanda exchanged apprehensive glances.

"You remember Detective Gleason," Powers said. "Please sit in these two chairs. I'll take the one next to the detective. There's water if you're thirsty."

"Thank you for coming," Gleason said, and then to Amanda. "First, I'm sorry about your husband, ma'am."

Amanda replied with a strained smile.

"Detective Powers said you have something you wanted to tell us," he continued.

"Yes, it concerns my husband.," Amanda said. "I've been in such a dither I don't know where to start. I'd be lost if it weren't for Candace to help me."

She smiled at Candace.

"Go ahead," Candace said. "It's all right."

"Drake was responsible for Lee's death," Amanda announced.

"Tell them what happened," Candace encouraged.

217

"It was an accident," Amanda explained. "Lee was keeping some things in the hangar and Drake wanted them out. Lee came to get them and they started arguing. Lee has a terrible temper and shoved Drake. Well, Drake shoved him back and Lee tripped and hit his head against something. He stopped breathing. Drake tried to give him CPR but it was too late."

"How long have you known this?" Gleason asked.

"Drake told me on the day he crashed that stupid airplane," she said. "Actually, he told both of us. Candace had come over for breakfast. You can imagine how frightening it must've been to hear something like that. I said he had to go to the police. He promised he would. He said he was scared before that no one would believe him but now he realized that was wrong. As soon as he got back, he said we'd all go together."

Gleason cut his eyes at Candace.

"Why didn't you two come forward sooner?" he demanded. "Why did you wait until now?"

"I was so upset I wasn't thinking clearly," Amanda said. "Neither of us was."

"Did he say what he did with Lee afterwards?" Gleason asked. "Obviously, he put him in the water somewhere. I'm just wondering how he got him there."

"No, he only told me how it'd happened."

Gleason turned to Candace.

"Miss Farrow, did Mr. Boynton ever mention anything about this to you before then?"

"No, I heard it for the first time that day. Once we finally got ourselves together, we decided we had to tell you. It's all so sad."

"Would you excuse Detective Powers and myself for a moment? We need to talk."

Powers and Gleason left the room.

"Let 'em sweat a little," Gleason grinned.

"What a crock!" Powers said. "They're lying their asses off."

Five minutes later they re-entered the interview room.

"Thank you for your patience," Gleason said, taking his seat. "Detective Powers has a few questions."

218

"Did you ever fly with your husband, Mrs. Boynton?" Powers asked

"No, I hate little airplanes. That was all Drake's thing. I wanted no part of it. And now I have to bury him."

"Miss Farrow, did you ever go up with him?"

"I don't like little planes either."

"I'm not a fan of them myself," Powers smiled, "but Drake Boynton obviously was. I can imagine him spending a lot of time at the airport babying that new airplane. You ever join him, Mrs. Boynton? Keep him company while he polished its wings or whatever?"

"No, like I told you, I have no interest in airplanes. I would've been bored to death there. Drake understood. He was okay with it."

"The hangar was his man cave," Candace added. "That was fine with us."

"So, you never went there either, Miss Farrow?"

"Not in a million years."

Powers paused.

"We have evidence that will prove otherwise," she said. "Do either of you want to change your story?"

Only shocked silence answered.

"Candace Farrow, you are under arrest for the murder of Lee Meadow," Powers said. "You have the right..."

"Don't say anything, honey!" Amanda interrupted.

Powers continued with reading Candace her rights and then turned to Amanda.

"Amanda Boynton, you are under arrest for accessory-after-the-fact in the homicide of Lee Meadow. You have the right ..."

Chapter 41

The two women had been taken to a holding cell at the police station. They'd be transported to the women's jail to await a bail hearing.

"Think that accessory charge on Boynton will stick?" Gleason asked.

He and Powers had returned to the detectives room.

"I don't know," Powers said. "I wanted to go with the strongest charge we could. DA will make that decision. I believe he'll at least charge her for hindering an investigation."

"Well, we've got forty-eight hours to get it done, otherwise they're released," Gleason agreed. "Actually, it's better than that. Weekend's coming up. We get an extra day. The two women get an extra day in the cooler, too."

"Nice to have gotten the results on those DNA swabs they took from the airplane," Powers said. "How sick. Meadow bouncing around in there. Even his body fluids were on the seat. That little shard the coroner found during the autopsy matched the broken windscreen, too. What I don't understand is why they undressed him."

"Laundry marks? Labels? Maybe some kind of disgracing act?"

"This whole thing didn't have to happen," Powers said. "Amanda Boynton's story about the fight at the hangar might actually be true. She just didn't mention Candace's part. And she is lying about when she first found out. I think she'd known for some time. But Drake and Candace could have pleaded self-defense if they'd called the police right then."

"I'm sure her lawyer will be on top of the self-defense angle," Gleason said.

"They just thought they were smarter than anyone else," Powers said. "Tight little group sticking together. Makes you almost sympathize with Lee Meadow."

"We need to include everything we've got for probable cause as to why we arrested them before we send the report to the district attorney," Gleason reminded her.

"I'm on it, sir."

~~~

As it turned out, the extra day wasn't of much help. Amanda Boynton was released. The district attorney decided that, while she probably was guilty of hindering, there simply wasn't enough evidence to prove it. He did note that should future information surface, she could be re-arrested. Candace Farrow was charged with first degree murder and held over for bail setting.

"I wonder what would've happened if George Ashby hadn't shown up when he did at the Boyntons," Powers said. "I'd just noticed that aviation magazine on the table. It would have been interesting to have seen where that might've taken us if we could've pursued it then. Of course, it helped us get there eventually."

She and Gleason were at work. They'd just received the news from the district attorneys' office.

"Spilt milk," Gleason said. "Forget it. As far as the Boynton woman goes, we simply couldn't make a case. Needed more than our word against hers. The DA had no choice but to cut her loose."

"I know. Still, it pisses me off. Same as with the security footage on the truck in Marathon. I'd bet anything that it was Drake Boynton picking up Candace Farrow. Hell, for all we know Amanda was also in the car."

"Forget that, too," Gleason said curtly. "We don't need any more speculation."

Powers was taken aback by that last remark.

"Speculation led us to the hangar, if I'm not mistaken, sir."

"You're right," Gleason admitted. "Didn't mean to anything. I'm as disappointed as you are that we didn't nail her. It'll be a sensational trial, that's for sure. Dead body dropped out of an airplane has a high ghoul factor. Should bring out all the loonies."

"How's the lieutenants test going. You ready for the interview?"

"Could be a one-horse race," Gleason said. "Sonny Breaks has his eye on the job."

"Halderman wouldn't let that happen," Powers said.

"Don't be surprised what with Breaks' heavy political juice."

~~~

"I love it when a lady invites me out for dinner," Jack said. "Better yet, when she chooses the restaurant."

Jack and Rachel had just been seated at the Cafe Sole'. She'd called him right after she had gotten home. It was the second phone call she'd made.

"I remembered you bringing me here," she said, smiling. "I had the hogfish. I believe you had shrimp."

"They do a good job with both. You going for it again?"

"I haven't decided," she said, tapping a finger on the table. "Maybe I'll surprise myself."

A pause settled between them.

"So, what's the occasion?" Jack asked. "I sense something's up."

"Oh, Jack, do you have ESP along with your other talents? Yes, something is up. Let's order some wine first."

Jack chose a nice chilled Chablis.

"Here's to your special occasion," he said, raising his glass.

"I hope you'll think so after I tell you."

"I have a feeling I already know."

Rachel turned her head aside.

"Damn," she said.

Jack smiled.

"You've made up your mind," he said.

"I'm to report at Fort Benning in three weeks. Jack, I'm so sorry."

"Why? It doesn't change anything between us. Just adds a little distance."

Rachel took his hand in hers.

"You're a very special person."

"Billy says I'm just a romantic."

❄ ❄ ❄

About the Author

Robert Coburn is originally from Norfolk, Virginia. After high school in Norfolk, he spent three years in the US Army as a helicopter crew chief stationed in Berlin, Germany. He returned home to attend college at Richmond Professional Institute (Now VCU) in Richmond, Virginia, where he earned a Bachelor of Science degree in Advertising. He also met his wife in Richmond while a student there.

Coburn has worked at major advertising agencies in New York and Los Angeles. His ads have won top awards both nationally and internationally. He is an instrument rated commercial pilot and plays saxophone. He and his wife now live in Carmel, California.

ABSOLUTELY AMAZING eBOOKS

AbsolutelyAmazingEbooks.com
or AA-eBooks.com

Made in the USA
San Bernardino, CA
10 September 2019